Interment
Published by The Conrad Press Ltd. in the United Kingdom 2025

Tel: +44(0)1227 472 874
www.theconradpress.com
info@theconradpress.com

ISBN 978-1-917673-63-1

Copyright © James Cole, 2025

All rights reserved.

Typesetting and Cover Design by: James Sadlier, jamessadlier@me.com
The Conrad Press logo was designed by Maria Priestley.

Printed and bound in Great Britain by Clays Ltd, Elcograf S.p.A

Thank you so much for reading my book!

INTERMENT
JAMES COLE

Truly hope you enjoy it.
Best wishes
James Cole

ACKNOWLEDGEMENTS

My children are my whole world. This book exists thanks to their love. My sons are called Finnley and Austin.

I wanted to ensure I left something permanent behind, especially for my children and any other children - or grandchildren - I may one day have.

Writing gives one the ability to do this, I believe.

There are too many people to thank for their help, support, and kind words.

Family is everything to me. I feel that they've had a huge impact on my writing.

People, whom I am proud to call my friends, have been the light in a dark tunnel – therefore, this novel is in honour of them.

I firmly believe that loving people is a gift. I wish to thank those loved ones the most.

I want to recognise all the great people in my life. I truly feel that without them, this journey of life would be quite unbearable.

Lastly, I wish to thank my publisher, The Conrad Press, who have made this publication possible. I look forward to writing many more novels for the avid reader to enjoy.

It's fundamental to me that one should take something away from my writing. However trivial it may seem, it means the world to me.

With my fondest regards and thanks.

PROLOGUE

March 1998

It was dark. To Jonny it felt like the darkest night he'd ever seen in his short ten years of life.

The wind howled around the small, one-storey house, as if it sat right in the eye of a tornado.

The rain ravaged the walls, the roof, the windows. Each drop sounded like a tiny unseen entity trying to enter through the glass to get to him. To have him.

The moon was full and round, but at this time it was hidden behind clouds, the glow barely visible. It was as if God had turned off the huge night-light in the sky.

He knew why. He was guilty. This was a punishment for his bad thoughts. His selfishness. He was also filled with an indescribable dread about the future. Something was coming and it was not good.

That's why this was happening. That's why the weather was getting worse. The wind howled louder, and the rain hit harder. The windows moaned and creaked, threatening to give way at any moment to let Mother Nature take him, her prize.

The attic was making noises too. He hated the attic. Any attic but this – his grandfather's was the worst. A bang. A scuffle. Almost like someone, or something, was up there waiting for him.

He squeezed his deep-blue eyes shut, forcing himself to calm down. A tear slowly ran down his cheek.

He was shaking. But no matter what, he would not investigate, and he would certainly not go to his grandfather's room.

His grandfather would just shout and then tease him: call him stupid, call him a baby, make him feel worthless, as always.

He missed his grandmother so much. Why had she gone? Why had she left him with the rest of his miserable excuse for a family? She was the only one that made them a family – a happy family. She was the absent glue that kept their family together, and happy. Normal.

Normal. Ha! Now that was just a distant memory.

He held back another urge to cry, to call for his mother, even though she was thousands of miles away on a holiday with his father. They had gone to Australia; he came to his grandfather's. What a deal.

Another bang from the attic drew him from his reverie. He tried to ignore it, but the bang was followed by a scratching noise that quickly became persistent. It sounded like a dog desperately looking for its bone under the couch where it couldn't quite reach, so all you could here was the sound of claws on wood.

The noise became louder, more vigorous, more violent.

Jonny squeezed his eyes shut again and didn't try to stop the tears that now ran freely down his cheeks, like the raindrops outside on the window.

Suddenly, all went silent.

No rain. No wind. No scratching from the attic. Nothing.

All he could hear was the quiet snoring from his grandfather's room.

But no, that wasn't all he could hear. He held his breath and listened hard. What was that?

It almost sounded like... whispering.

He slowly began to raise his head to look up at the ceiling, from where the whispers came.

As his eyes looked up, in his peripheral vision he saw something move past the window.

He jerked his head right and stared through the glass.

He could feel his heart thumping in his chest as if it was about to burst through his ribcage. He had seen something; he was sure of it.

It had been white, or at least he thought it was white – maybe grey?

He let out a breath that he hadn't noticed he'd been holding. A warm mist of air escaped his lips. The room had become freezing cold: like ice, like a morgue. He began to breathe quickly and shallowly in panic.

The more he breathed, the more mist he saw expelled from his lungs, emerging from his mouth.

The whispers again. He shifted his gaze back to the ceiling, scrutinizing it as if it was about to come to life and open up, letting go of whatever misery was up there waiting for him, watching him.

As he once again focused on the window, he could see a figure standing on the other side of the glass... Jonny stared and realised with horror that it was not alone.

Outside, behind the misty glass, stood eight or maybe ten greyish-white figures.

It was hard to see through the increasingly misty, wet panes of glass, but there were silhouettes.

They all looked the same. No, not the same, but similar. He couldn't make out their features, as their heads were bowed, but he knew they wore no clothes. They were naked.

The figure closest to the window seemed to have no feet, no legs. He did a double take and saw that it did have legs, but those of an animal. That could not be!

He was entranced by these beings. They had not moved a muscle. Was he scared? Yes, out of his mind, but somehow, he had to see more. He slowly began to creep off the sofa bed and tentatively put a foot on the freezing-cold carpet.

It was wet, and so cold that he snatched his foot back from the floor.

Just then, the door of the lounge, where minutes previously he had been sleeping, flew open.

His grandfather stood in the doorway, in the shadows, not moving a muscle.

Jonny was petrified. He could not breathe. He stole looks between the abominations outside and his grandfather. His eyes shot between the two, like he was watching a ping-pong match.

His grandfather slowly entered the room, floating, gliding almost, like a ghost.

A dull light seemed to be emanating from the beings outside, illuminating his grandfather just for a few seconds.

In those few seconds Jonny's heart was in his throat. His grandfather's eyes were completely white, and his face was contorted in a vicious snarl, or maybe it was an evil grin.

Jonny shook all over. He was tempted to hide under the blanket but didn't – he just stared. The moon began to peak out from the clouds. His grandfather sat in his usual seat, and began to stare with his white eyes at the television screen, even though it was switched off.

There was complete silence. Jonny held his breath, more from terror than anything else.

Suddenly his grandfather's head snapped sharply right and stared at him.

The old man's eyes were no longer white, they were totally black – as black as the dark night outside. Black and empty, evil even.

In a deep, rasping, unfamiliar voice, his grandfather said, 'Boy... soon you will join us...' erupting into a sudden fit of coughs, blood beginning to run from his eyes.

Jonny looked at his grandfather and realised that his eyes again appeared normal, except for the blood that poured from them like rivers. Then, suddenly, as quickly as it had begun, the bleeding stopped.

Jonny's grandfather just stared at him with a bewildered look on his face. There was nothing outside, and no noise. There was now uninterrupted light coming from the full moon, clearly visible through the clear, unblemished window. The cold had gone, the temperature normal, comfortable even. There was no blood, no sign of it. What had just happened?

'Sorry, son, must have... must have fallen asleep again watching the box. I... I'll see you in the morning,' his grandfather said as he got up and left the room.

Jonny was all alone again, but calm – there was no feeling of the impending doom that had been lurking just moments ago.

He lay his head back down on the pillow and stared out at the moon. 'God help me,' he whispered as he drifted off into a restless sleep.

CHAPTER 1

Jonny cursed as the steaming hot tea burnt his tongue – it felt as if it was starting to dissolve from the boiling-hot liquid, like acid stripping paint. He could never wait. If he just blew, then drank gingerly as his mother told him, this daily tongue torture would cease to exist.

But like most things in Jonny's life, impulse and a desire for everything to happen instantly was his undoing.

He reached out for some more sugar to try and sweeten his tea and hopefully brighten his dreary Monday morning.

His hand shook slightly as he poured the tiny white grains into his mug. He watched them disappear to the bottom of the liquid as if they never existed, stirred it and sighed.

Why? Why had it happened again? In the early hours of the morning again – between two and three am, was it?

Tomorrow was his birthday. Why did it have to happen the day before that? A day he always looked forward to, as he got to take a week off work and enjoy himself.

So why had that damn dream come back to haunt him the day before his birthday, making him a nervous, shaking wreck!

It had been exactly the same before, all those years ago. Identical. He had remembered everything from that dream, and it was just the same as last night's. Well, nearly the same...

When he was a kid, those words that his grandfather had said... well, whatever was in his grandfather at the time had said: 'Boy... soon you will join us...'

He remembered those words in his mind like they were engraved in stone. He had tried for years to forget them, but it just wasn't possible.

In the end he had decided to just live with the memory, deal with it.

But the thing was, this time in his dream the words were: 'Jonathan, you will soon join us. The twenty-fifth Sabbath approaches.'

What did that mean? Why had the words changed, and why could he never finish the dream?

So many questions. He put the lava-hot tea down on the counter and rubbed his bearded face roughly, trying to wake himself up.

His deep blue eyes were weary from the poor night's sleep. He sighed and stretched, his T-shirt riding up to reveal a lean, strong body.

His skin was blemish free, his curly, chocolate hair unkept but always managing to fall in a perfect, styled position when he got out of bed. He was lucky that way. His strong jaw line and friendly smile had made him attractive to the opposite sex, even if it was in a somewhat rugged way, and he knew it. Jonny was the rugged type really, and although he was aware he held attractive qualities, he was by no means full of himself – he had enough self-confidence to enjoy life, but that was as far as it went.

He appreciated the interest from women and the feeling was often mutual.

However, currently he was keen to continue focusing on himself, and happy to pay himself some much-needed attention for a short while.

He picked up the mug of tea once again and took a sip more carefully, still lost in his thoughts.

He was shocked out of his contemplation by a voice right behind him, mere inches away from his right ear.

'Hey, dude,' the voice said from behind him.

He jumped. 'Doug, what the hell?' Jonny exclaimed, barely saving his tea from a disastrous end.

'You know it's your birthday tomorrow, buddy, maybe we should try find someone to finally take you off my hands,' his friend said with a smirk.

'Well, I'd like to see you try and pay for this place on your own, dickhead, or that new chick you're seeing. How much do you reckon she earns jerking people off all day anyway?' said Jonny, laughing.

'Hey, screw you!' Doug said whilst grinning, 'She's a sports therapist, you prick!'

'Yea? Well, when are we going to see some rent money, man? She practically lives here, and it should go three ways!' Jonny said, whilst stirring yet another spoon of sugar into his tea. It might be cool enough finally, he thought absentmindedly.

'I wanted to talk to you about that actually, Jonny,' Doug said, all trace of his jovial tone now gone.

'Oh yea? What's up?' Jonny said with a little concern in his voice. He didn't think his friend noticed his unease, but Jonny sure felt it.

'Well, me and Kate have been together for like six months now and we think it's time to, like, live together as a proper couple,' Doug said, eyeing Jonny with some caution.

'Ah I see. So, you wanna get your own place with her?' Jonny replied.

'Umm... actually, we were hoping to have this place to ourselves and maybe you could... move out?' Doug said quietly, like a child asking for a gift that was way beyond their parents' bank balance.

Jonny was stunned. He replied: 'Seriously, Doug? The day before my birthday and you drop this shit on me now? I thought we were best mates man. I mean, really? It was your idea to bring me up here, forgetting to tell me that the rent on this place would be virtually all my problem!' As he spoke, he walked to the other side of the kitchen and shoved some bread into the toaster, a little too firmly.

Jonny whirled around as he felt his friend place a hand on his shoulder, Doug saying in an almost desperate tone: 'We are best mates, dude, and I love you, man, but I love her too. You're twenty-five tomorrow, bro, and I'm twenty-seven next month. We're growing up and I wanna seal the deal whilst I still can. I know you've been single for, like twelve months or something, but you got all your family down south waiting for you. I haven't really got anyone anywhere anymore.'

Jonny looked at him for a second. Doug's dark brown eyes were pleading with him. He swore he could see tears in them. He looked so innocent, with his schoolboy good looks... and charm to boot. His neat blond hair hung low over his brow, making him resemble a Golden Labrador puppy.

Jonny couldn't do anything to hurt his friend, even if it meant living alone again.

'You're a jerk off,' he said to Doug with a grin.

'Yeah yeah, why don't you blow me,' Doug said laughing. Then he was on Jonny, embracing him in an enormous bear hug. Both men were fairly large, Jonny, around six-feet tall, and bulky – Doug was similar, but maybe slightly taller.

'Thanks, man. I love you,' Doug said and wiped a tear from his eye. He then ran off upstairs, to tell Kate (Jonny presumed) the good news.

Jonny sighed and looked out the window. He then slinked off to the bathroom and began to brush his teeth. Whilst he slowly massaged his gums with the new electric toothbrush he'd received for his early birthday gift from his aunty, he contemplated that dream again – the changes in it, the different words, the significance of the prayer he had said over and over again as a kid. 'Protect me' – had it all been for nothing? If so, why now?

'This is stupid,' he said to himself, and began to wash his mouth out with the cool running water. He froze when he looked up. He began to shake all over. In front of him, his breath shot out in cold clouds like it was winter. The mirror misted up, and to his utter amazement letters began to form on the glass. Now they were words. Now those words formed a sentence: 'See you soon, Jonathan.'

CHAPTER 2

Jonny slowly, almost begrudgingly, stepped out of his car. He stretched up high to the sky and his gaze lingered for a while on the darkening clouds. It was one hell of a drive from Northern Scotland down south to his parents' home.

'Ugh, I thought it wouldn't rain today,' he said to no one in particular. He shut the door, grabbed his bag from the back seat and locked the car.

He slowly walked up the steps to his parents' modest two-bedroom, nineteenth century terraced house. It was a nice house, with beautiful Cotswold stone walls that always made him think of quality and class.

The big gold knocker clanged loudly against the freshly painted bright-red door.

'Hey, son!' were the first words out of his father's mouth before a bone-crushing handshake, followed by a typical man hug.

'Hey, Pa,' Jonny said, as he squeezed past his father to kiss his mother on the cheek.

'Had a good day?' his mother asked excitedly.

'Usual, Mum. All good though. Work is good and looks like we're safe for a couple more years yet.'

'Good to hear! I hope you're looking forward to the barbie tonight. Your sister and the kids will be here soon along with your Auntie. Are your friends still coming?' his dad queried.

'Couple are, not many, I didn't want to make it a huge thing really,' Jonny replied.

'Go get yourself comfy in the guest room, get ready and by then people will be here I'm sure,' his mother said.

Jonny smiled at both of them, tiredly but warmly, and

slowly climbed up the stairs to the guest room. He unpacked a few things and then just sat on the side of the bed and slowly took some much-needed deep breaths. He listened to his mother clatter around in the kitchen. Thanks to the open window, he could hear his father outside, who had just lit the grill, and was already hassling his mother with questions about where the cooking utensils were, which of course had been moved since he last used them.

With a sharp intake of breath, he was up and unpacking, ready to change.

Five minutes later he was downstairs feeling fresh and ready to eat and drink himself into a coma.

They always liked to do birthday stuff the night before running into his birthday, that way they could celebrate both days, and now that he was older, have a drink when it had gone twelve am.

'Get this down you, son,' his dad said as he handed him an ice-cold beer.

'Will do, Pa,' Jonny said, as knocked back half the beer in one huge gulp.

He clinked his bottle with his father's and said, 'Here's to a good night and a good twenty-fifth year!'

'Definitely!' his father said.

CHAPTER 3

Jonny slammed his palm against the steering wheel of the Jeep.

He sat at the red light, staring at it. He bored into it with his anger, hoping it would change its mind and instantly turn green, which of course it didn't.

The wind howled around outside the Grand Cherokee. Leaves blew mercilessly against the windscreen as the wipers did their best to clear the glass. Torrents of rain lashed down on the car. Jonny looked up for an instant, as a flash of lightning illuminated the cabin through the panoramic glass roof.

Suddenly there was a huge rumble. Jonny swore he could feel the thunder's resounding rumble in his teeth.

He continued to sit with the Jeep in 'Park' at the temporary traffic lights. No other cars had come up behind him and no cars were passing from the other direction.

'Probably bloody broken knowing my luck,' he muttered to himself.

The next track from his phone loaded up and pounded through the Jeep's sound system – a new rock band he had discovered recently with some serious metal twists. He turned up the volume and the car shook with the bass and crazy guitar riffs.

Why was there even a set of temporary lights here? He couldn't see a reason for them, and this road was rarely used. It was a winding country road with a cliff climbing high into the night sky on one side and a steeply sloping forest on the other.

Far below the forest was a rushing river, which he

remembered, as he had occasionally used this road before for work.

'Screw this,' he said angrily as he slammed the Jeep into 'Drive' and accelerated hard past the red light. He looked warily through the rain to make sure nobody was coming and deduced that he would be safe, as both sides of the road seemed to be clear of any roadworks or damage.

Suddenly a massive clap of thunder and a flash of lightning rattled the SUV. It felt as if it was right on top of him – it was so bright he was dazzled by it. He could see little stars as his eyes tried to adjust to the foreboding dark outside again.

'Why am I out here?' he questioned, 'I know why... God damn Doug!' he replied to himself, harshly.

A complete waste of one of his holiday days. The day after his damn birthday and he was back up in Scotland, shopping for a one-bedroom apartment to rent.

The day had started badly, and like the properties he had viewed, had got worse from there on. Jonny was stressed, as he knew he needed an apartment near to the office. The old apartment *was* technically the office, so he couldn't have got closer to work than that!

Now he was on his way to the last viewing of the day. This one was only available to see at half past six, which meant it was now pitch black.

It was in the arse end of nowhere too. He questioned why he was even going to see this place – it was too expensive for what it was and too far out of town.

He looked at the sat-nav screen and it was recalculating the route, then said 'return to the route'.

'Give me a break!' Jonny shouted angrily at the heavens.

He let his foot drop down hard on the accelerator and the big V6 diesel engine rumbled angrily as the Jeep dropped down a gear, then another and accelerated quickly. The powerful engine propelled the big truck forwards, the rev counter touching the red line before the automatic gearbox selected the next gear.

He eased off the accelerator as he calmed down. A frown crossed his features, followed by confusion. Jonny eased off the accelerator further and then slowly began to brake. His eyes focused on the bright light ahead. 'What the...' Jonny said out loud, as the truck slowed to a crawl.

Just ahead, on the right side of the road was a clearing. Perched in between the trees, just before the steep drop off the side of the hill, was a diner. At least that's what the red glowing neon sign above it stated.

'Halfway Diner?' Jonny questioned. 'Am I high?' he said to himself with a smirk.

Jonny had been down this road before in the past twelve months and didn't remember a clearing, let alone an old-school diner.

He pulled off the road into the dirt car park and stared up at the massive, glowing neon sign. Next to that was an obnoxiously large American flag. It dominated what was a very loud front to a relatively small building.

He parked the Jeep and killed the engine, then just sat there, completely confused. He stared around his surroundings. There were a couple other cars in the car park – a 1980s Capri and next to that an ancient-looking Rolls-Royce, perhaps from the 1960s or even the 1950s.

He was amazed that there were customers here at all, considering the location and the truly awful weather. He looked at the grimy windows and struggled to see anything, especially with the wipers no longer arcing across the windscreen.

He looked more closely and could see shadows inside the diner, he was sure of it. People were milling around... lots of them.

He noticed someone by the door – they slowly walked past and looked outside at him, or at least at his truck. It was difficult to make out their features, as there was another, smaller, bright neon sign on the door. It read: 'We Are Open, come on in!' It was written in an overly jovial font, and flashed slowly on and off.

Jonny grabbed the truck's door handle and then stopped. He stared at it and then back at the diner. He couldn't see any shadows moving now, but he was certain plenty of people were in there.

He sighed and pushed the door open. He grabbed it again sharply as he dropped out of the driver's seat – the wind had tried to take it clean off the truck, and he'd grabbed it just in time.

He couldn't believe this weather. It was torrential out here and the wind howled, forming a vortex around him. He pulled his coat tightly around his body, almost hugging it to himself, and squinting as he walked into the storm, towards the entrance to the diner.

He stepped up onto the stoop and was thankful that the overhang from the roof protected him from the worst of the weather. He grabbed the door handle and stopped. He couldn't understand why, but he just froze. His stomach did a somersault. He felt nervous, he felt... afraid. What the hell was wrong with him? Jonny was a social person and had never been shy of anything really, not even losing his virginity.

He shook his head to try and clear it, and began to pull the heavy door. It slowly moved, and as he increased the pressure it suddenly popped open.

He stood there looking in. It was indeed busy.

There were twenty-five, maybe thirty customers inside and several servers running around. The hum of conversation filled his ears.

He stepped onto the welcome mat and the door slammed shut behind him with a merry jingle from the bell hanging above it.

The heater above the entrance blew warm, clear air onto him, like a breezy summer day.

He now looked up, as he had busied himself removing his soaked coat as soon as the door had shut behind him.

Music was playing somewhere; he hadn't noticed at first. It was an old Elvis track if he was not mistaken. Apart from that, there was no noise. Not a whisper.

Every single person in the diner had gone silent, and they had all turned to look at him.

CHAPTER 4

Jonny stood there awkwardly. He scanned the scene in front of him before looking down at his sodden jeans – the ripped design had allowed water to soak through onto his skin. His battered Vans were not holding up much better either – he looked at one, then the other and then lifted his gaze back to the room.

He took a mental step back. He couldn't believe it. All the patrons of the diner were now completely ignoring him, as they had when he first entered.

Not one person stared at him any longer, with their slack faces and judging eyes. It was as if the incident had never happened. He questioned how sound his mind was – had he imagined the whole thing?

They were all engrossed in conversation, or eating, or drinking coffee.

Jonny took another few steps forward and came to a halt in front of a small sign reading: 'Welcome! Please wait to be seated!'

He had barely finished looking at the sign when a cheerful voice said: 'Hi!'.

Jonny snapped his eyes up to meet the gaze of a somewhat plump, but friendly looking man probably in his early forties, whose white shirt didn't quite fit, with a corner at the front sticking out where it had become untucked. Jonny could see beads of sweat on the man's forehead. A name badge on the man's shirt stated that his name was Ray.

'You're here for a table,' Ray said. It was a statement not a question.

Jonny raised an eyebrow, but before he could say anything,

Ray spoke again.

'Name's Ray, I'll be looking after you. Anything you need, give me a holler. Follow me!' he said in a tired, but happy and genuinely friendly voice.

'Uh OK, thanks,' Jonny said to Ray's back, as he had already turned and was busy marching down one of the diner's aisles, Jonny moving quickly to keep up.

Jonny was surprised at Ray's accent – it was American, Mid-West if he was not mistaken. He seemed a nice guy, maybe overly happy and quite camp, but very friendly.

'This is you,' said Ray, pointing to a small booth, with space for two, plus an extra chair.

'Thanks, Ray,' said Jonny, 'Uh, say, Ray, umm, I've lived in this area for quite some time and have never spotted this place. Is it new?' while thinking to himself it sure didn't look it.

Ray looked at him with a faltering smile, but before Jonny could study it any longer, the full smile was back like nothing had happened.

'Always been here, friend! Just gotta spot it!' Ray replied happily.

Before Jonny could say anything else, Ray motored through the usual few quick points about the diner and its service: 'So yeah, you know where the bathroom is, where the jukebox is and of course me!' He finished with: 'I'll start you with a coffee and come back once you're ready to order.' With that, he turned and rushed off to the kitchen counter.

Jonny looked around bemused. He stared briefly down at the menu and then looked around the diner.

It was dated, sure, but it was homely enough. It was clean and had plenty of space.

The windows were grubby on the outside, especially the front (he had noticed when he entered), but that was probably due to the weather.

Another song started on the jukebox. It was some old country-and-western song that Jonny had never heard – not the sort of thing you expect to hear in Britain really, but probably in keeping with the American flavour of the diner.

Jonny smirked and said to himself, 'Not the sort of joint you'd find in Britain either!'

The faux red leather under his legs and butt squeaked from his wet jeans. He sighed and sunk into the comfy seat.

'Here we are! Ready to order something to eat?' Ray said, surprising Jonny out of his dreaming.

'Sure... listen, Ray, I haven't looked at the menu, can I just have a simple sandwich?' Jonny said.

'What sort of sandwich?' replied Ray, with a smile.

'Um, I'm easy, man, what have you got?' Jonny said wryly.

'Pretty much anything! We cater for everyone here – all shapes, sizes and backgrounds! Special is the New York Deli sandwich with fries, and a unicorn shake. A-Ma-Zing, I swear!' Ray said with a giggle and a smile.

'Sure,' Jonny said with a tired smile and a little laugh of his own.

'Coming right up, Jonny!' Ray said, and shot off towards the kitchen yet again.

Jonny relaxed back into his seat.

He listened to the chit-chatter of busy conversation around him. He tapped the table with his fingers to the now more modern 'You Oughta Know' by Alanis Morrisette.

As he closed his eyes and heard the rain lashing down on the window, he hummed along to the song.

Suddenly his eyes slowly opened, and he frowned deeply. 'What the?' Jonny said to himself, confused, 'I never told that guy my name!'

CHAPTER 5

The sandwich was average. It looked amazing, and Jonny supposed that's what made it worse than it was – it was just OK but looked like it should be the best sandwich ever. 'What a shame,' he sighed to himself.

The fries were overdone and the shake... well it tasted good, but was like drinking water – not what Jonny thought of when you said milkshake. God knows what the flavour was, but it was interesting.

He sighed again and pushed the plate away, half finished.

The behemoth sandwich looked like a half-mauled loaf of bread just sitting there.

He looked around again, deciding to do a little people-watching.

He certainly wasn't in a rush to leave, considering the weather had not let up one iota.

As Jonny paid more attention to his fellow patrons in the diner, he began to appreciate that Ray's comment on all shapes and sizes didn't do the place justice.

Every type of person was there, from every ethnic background, every size and every style.

People were dressed crazily! Some wore similar clothes to himself – ripped jeans and a sweater – but others wore suits that looked almost Victorian. Some looked like rednecks just coming off an oil field.

Jonny did a double take when he noticed one guy with slicked-back hair wearing shades, a Hawaiian shirt and swimming shorts – yes, swimming shorts!

'What the hell is going on here?' Jonny said to no one in particular.

Just then, a woman rushed past him towards the bathroom. She seemed to be upset, as he could hear her sobbing. She was wearing what could only be described as a wedding dress.

'I have officially entered Nutsville, I swear to God,' Jonny mused with an ironic laugh.

He looked over at the kitchen counter and saw Ray having a heated conversation with the only chef working that night. There were hand gestures from the chef and eye-rolling from Ray.

Jonny picked up one of the cold fries and popped it in his mouth. He thought about Ray as he chewed. 'I didn't tell him my name,' he thought to himself again.

When Ray had dropped off the meal, he had been in such a rush that Jonny didn't get a word in before he was off again.

This time he just called him 'buddy'. He didn't imagine it did he? Of course not. He wasn't crazy like half the lot in here.

'Fuck it,' he mumbled to no one in particular, drawing a line under it. He got up and headed for the bathroom.

Luckily there were both male and female bathrooms, as he didn't want to have to wait awkwardly outside a single bathroom, waiting for the depressed bride to reappear.

He pushed the door open and went inside. Mercifully, it was empty.

One of the strip lights on the ceiling blinked off frequently, and the room smelt worse than a festival Portaloo.

He decided he would not risk entering the cubicle, and headed for the urinal. He unbuttoned his jeans and began to urinate.

He closed his eyes and sighed with relief, not having noticed how much he needed a piss.

'Nice dick! Want me to suck it when you're done?' came a woman's voice to the left of him. He jumped back in surprise, shoving himself back into his boxers and raising his hands in a gesture of 'easy now'.

He looked at the woman, and realised it was the depressed bride. She looked to be around her early twenties – probably pretty under all that hair and running makeup. Her eyes were surrounded by dark rims of mascara, and they were red from crying.

She stepped forward slowly with a smirk on her face.

'No one gives a shit, and I know you want me... come on, whip it out and I'll give you the best head you've ever had, baby,' she said to him in a quiet, girly voice – she was clearly trying to sound as alluring as possible.

She pulled at the top of the wedding dress, sliding it halfway down her arms so that her breasts fell out. They were large and firm, and heaved with her breathing that seemed rapid with excitement.

Jonny took another step back, feeling very exposed. She stepped closer to him so that they were only inches apart.

She looked up at him, into his eyes. Her big brown eyes were pretty, once he looked past the mascara rings and running makeup. Her blonde hair was matted to her forehead, but he couldn't see much more, as she wore a veil that was flipped back.

She smiled at him and reached out. She grabbed at his crotch.

'N... no,' Jonny whispered, but his resolve was faltering as her hand encircled his penis. It was growing by the second, and then popped over the top of his boxers like a jack-in-the-box.

'Goddamned dicks, they never think about the consequences,' he thought to himself. This was ridiculous. He wasn't going to do anything with this woman, she was clearly upset and slightly deranged, but his excitable manhood was not helping.

It was fully erect now and her hand was no longer encircling it on the outside of his boxers, but was gripping it firmly, flesh on flesh.

In his mind, he rolled his eyes at the joke of a situation he found himself in. Talk about being caught with your pants down, he thought. He almost laughed out loud.

'Hey, e… easy, hun, I'm not here for any of that,' he stuttered quietly.

The woman smiled innocently, fluttered her eyelashes at him and grabbed one of her breasts that was protruding proudly. She bit her bottom lip, trying to be seductive. It was kind of working, Jonny thought sadly. She pinched her nipple and giggled as it became erect, pointing in Jonny's direction.

'Don't be shy, babe, wouldn't you want to screw a bride on her wedding day?' she said casually with a lopsided grin.

Jonny was left open mouthed – he didn't know what to do.

Before he could say anything, she took her hand off him and moved it to her other breast, squeezing them together. Her impressive cleavage was meant to tantalize Jonny, but he was getting more and more concerned with every moment.

'This girl is going to go crazy if I tell her to get out and leave me alone,' he thought.

She placed one of her hands on the side of the sink, gripping it, then slowly, with a big smile, she began to kneel. Jonny looked around desperately, with panic in his eyes. There was no way out of this, she had backed him into a wall, literally.

He had to decide what to do. Either risk upsetting a potentially psychotic bride (who seemed to have been left at the alter earlier that day) or let her give him head. His dick had definitely made up its mind, but Jonny's conscience knew he would feel guilty taking advantage of this girl, who clearly had issues.

Just then, as he decided to persuade his dick back into his boxers, the door flew open.

It was Ray. He looked at the scene in front of him. He eyed Jonny and then the girl.

After a split second of holding his breath, Jonny said: 'Uh... Ray... I...,' but Ray cut him off.

'No need to explain, Jonny, this one has been harassing my male customers all night! Come on, Lucy, up you get, let's get you back to your seat. You leave this nice man alone, OK?' he said to her kindly.

As he did so, he bent down and slowly lifted her back up with him, his arm around her.

She looked angry initially, and then a frown crossed her face. She looked to be deep in thought, or was it confusion?

'S... sorry, Ray, I just wanted a bit of fun... the new guy's hot,' Lucy said, looking at Ray, Jonny now completely ignored.

Before Jonny could respond to this, wanting to know what the hell the 'new guy' comment was about, and the fact that Ray had again used his name, they had both turned and walked out of the bathroom.

Jonny was alone again.

He looked at the mirror, which had smear marks all over it. He tried to wipe it and focus on himself. He took a few breaths and washed his face.

'What... the... actual... fuck?' he said to the mirror. Then he laughed to himself. The mirror did not reply.

He clapped his hands together in an attempt to draw a line under an increasingly odd night. He washed his hands thoroughly, feeling rather dirty, and headed for the door.

He walked outside, expecting to see people looking at him as a result of the commotion from the bathroom, but no one paid him the slightest bit of attention.

He sighed and headed for his seat.

He sat down, not paying attention other than noticing that the sandwich and shake had now been cleared away.

He sat back and looked up. He took a sharp breath and stared in disbelieve. Sat on the other bench was a pretty girl – a girl that Jonny knew.

CHAPTER 6

Jonny let out a breath that he didn't notice he had been holding. It came out slow and ragged, like an old person's death rattle. He was in complete shock. He just sat there, mouth open, staring wide-eyed. His usually rugged, but attractive features were creased into what could be perceived as fear, or confusion, maybe both. Then he spoke: 'Autumn... you... you're dead.'

She smiled at him, sadly. She said nothing, just looked at him and placed a hand on top of his.

They both sat there in silence, looking at each other for what felt like the longest time.

Even the weather seemed to have subsided slightly, as if it knew this was an impossible and incredibly emotional moment for Jonny. It almost seemed like respect was being paid, as mourners would bow their heads at a funeral.

Finally, Autumn broke the silence and spoke: 'Jonny. Yes, it's me. I know, it's a lot to take in.' She raised her hands up as she spoke, to emphasise the seriousness of the situation.

The diner seemed to have quietened down somewhat too, and the hum of activity was now more of a murmur.

The jukebox kicked in with a favourite of Jonny's – a favourite of theirs.

'Mama I'm Coming Home' by Ozzy Osbourne had begun to play. The rock ballad meant a lot to both of them and seemed to fit the mood perfectly.

'You remember when we first listened to this song together?' Autumn said to him with a quizzical look that turned into a cheeky smile.

Jonny sat in silence, still dumbstruck, then answered:

'Yeah.' He coughed, and let a lump in his throat pass, wiping watery eyes that begun to well up like dripping taps.

'When we decided to go all the way for the first time on that camping trip with the boys... and of course, Katie and Laura,' he mused, his stare unfocused as if he was staring back into the memories of happier times.

'It was the first time I'd ever heard Ozzy Osbourne, and I knew you loved his music... I only knew him from the TV show!' She laughed, and shook her head with the fond memory.

'I loved it right away though, we listened to that song on repeat until your little iPod battery died, remember?' she continued.

'God yeah... the old iPod from my dad... It didn't even have a colour screen! Those were the days,' he said dreamily.

He shook his head, and then focused on Autumn.

'What is this, Autumn? What is going on? How are you here? Nothing makes sense anymore. I've had the worst day, and some crazy bride just tried to suck me off in the men's bathroom... I need answers,' he said to her firmly, with pleading eyes. He looked like a puppy desperate for its treat, but for him it was the need for an answer, an answer to everything.

'Like I said, babe... it's a lot to take in. I'm sorry you have to go through this... I'm sorry you're even here... I hoped you never would be. You're an amazing guy; well, you were when I knew you. I'm so sorry. I'm sorry you have to experience this, and I am sorry I left you. I never wanted to. You must believe me,' she pleaded.

Her eyes were searching as she stared at him. Those big green eyes he remembered so well. Her long, dark brown hair, still as beautiful and flowing as it had always been.

Autumn was petite, but the subtle lines of an elegant female form were clearly noticeable.

Jonny knew she had beautiful long, tanned legs, the best ass he'd ever seen, and a tight, well-toned body that was also always beautifully tanned. She was lucky like that. Whenever they went to the lake with their group of friends, she would strip off to her bikini and he would gawk at her figure and her lovely tan that seemed as attracted to her as he was.

One time at the beach, before they had even started dating, they had just shared their first kiss on the coach ride. All their friends were there too and had made a big thing about it. Autumn was quite embarrassed, but Jonny didn't care. He was so happy, and knew that kiss had meant something to both of them. He was on cloud nine – screw his stupid mates, they were just jealous!

When they all got off the coach, the wind and sand hit them in the face straight away. It was the summer holidays but in typical British fashion, it was windy. At least it was hot, thank God.

Once they were set up, Jonny and Autumn had gone into the water to swim. They were having a great time, splashing about, swimming, doing underwater summersaults and generally hoofing about.

Laura, one of Autumn's best friends was in the water too, with Brad, her boyfriend and, subsequently, Jonny's best friend.

For some unknown reason, Brad thought it would be funny to lift Laura and chuck her through the water. She screamed when he picked her up, and came up from a wave spluttering but laughing.

Brad was floating close to Autumn, and as her back was to him, he decided to do the same to her. In a split second she was in the air and then splashed back down into the water.

Jonny had been concerned until she popped up a second later.

She laughed for a second and then realised her bikini top had ridden right up, exposing her breasts.

She went from laughing to shock and anger at Brad within a second.

Jonny, being just fifteen at the time, stood there with his mouth hanging open... a fish could have jumped out of the water and slapped him in the face, and he wouldn't have batted an eyelid. He was mesmerised by Autumn's breasts, and couldn't believe how big they were considering she was also just fifteen.

That had been the end of their swim that day, but they had laughed and partied on the beach until it was time to catch the last coach back to town and their respective homes.

Jonny was shaken from his memories by Autumn placing her hand on his again, a look of concern visible in her pretty features.

'Are you OK?' she asked.

'Yeah, just a flash-back to that time at the beach where I saw your boobs for the first time,' he laughed.

She laughed too, and then focused on him again. She took a deep breath.

The song finished, and another began to play. It was an old pop song that Jonny had never heard before.

'Jonny,' she said seriously. 'You're right, I... I am dead... and so are you.'

CHAPTER 7

Jonny stared out of the window. He didn't look at Autumn, nor did he move, not one single muscle. He just stared out the window into the howling night; so dark, dark like his mind and soul, or at least that's how he felt at that moment in time.

The darkness he was staring into did not make him question what Autumn had just told him.

Oddly, he wasn't even thinking about it. Instead, his mind was being drawn back to the worst night of his life.

Turning eighteen had been a big deal for Jonny and he was keen to enjoy that year's prom in full, and with no more issues over being able to drink, it was going to be awesome.

His first prom had been a bit of a let-down, with watered-down alcohol and a jealous date who was not a fan of Autumn, who he ended up spending most of the night with.

He and Autumn had been laughing and chatting most of the evening, but Jonny had known it wasn't *his* date he was enjoying his time with. Autumn was there with someone else.

At that time, they had been on a break for a few months – they had mutually decided to try being just friends again after nearly two years of dating.

That hadn't lasted long though, as they didn't find the fun and enjoyment in others that they both secretly expected, and that they had always found in each other.

So, before the next year's prom, they were fully back together, and loving life.

As it was their last prom, they wanted to go out with a bang before university.

Jonny, Brad and a few of his other closest friends decided to go in matching vintage-style tuxes, which although looked hilarious, were also pretty cool and suited them.

Jonny had gone all out and gone for the full American style – the stretch limo, the corsage, the planned after-party, the lot.

The prom had been truly epic, from the moment he had collected Autumn in the limo with the others, eight of them in total.

Autumn had looked truly sensational when he had collected her at the front door to her parents' house. She looked so elegant and so grown up, a real adult, which is how he felt about himself that night too.

He had placed a hand on hers and attached the corsage, then he had walked her to the limo, placing a hand softly on the small of her back, which was open to the warm night's breeze, as her dress was backless.

She had smiled at him during the limo ride, that perfect smile with those beautiful, gleaming white teeth. She looked so happy, and so was Jonny.

They had enjoyed several dances during the night, but mainly enjoyed being in a group, drinking, laughing and revelling in each other's company, knowing this would be the last official time they did so.

The last dance had been a particularly memorable one for both of them.

They had slow danced to a dreary, mushy song that for the life of him, Jonny couldn't name. He had been so engrossed in that moment at that time. They had been engrossed in each other and in love.

Autumn had laid her head on his shoulder, and they had slowly moved around the dance floor, bodies pressed against each other, a smile playing on Jonny's face as he hugged her tight to him.

They had plans. They were both going to apply to the same university, along with Brad and another of Autumn's friends, Jenna. It wasn't long until they would receive their A-Level results, and they were both confident they could go together and stay together.

They both knew that people dreamed of having that one person that makes them feel special every day, from the moment they meet them. They also knew that rarely actually happened, but for Jonny it had, and he was certain Autumn felt the same, as she had virtually said so herself.

The last dance had finished, and they had all climbed into the stretch limo which took them to Brad's parents' house.

Brad came from a wealthy family with a big house in the country. His parents were easy going and had allowed him to have a post-prom party this year for nearly everyone from their year who attended the prom.

The after-party had been epic, drinking games, pranks, a little weed and, of course, more dancing and general fooling around.

Near the end of the night, Jonny and Autumn had decided to take a walk and clear their heads from the drink and smoky atmosphere.

Although the party was winding down, it was still bouncing, so the walk was a welcome distraction.

They walked through the house's grounds and headed past a water fountain. Autumn removed her corsage, held it between both hands and closed her eyes tight like a little girl making her birthday wish, before dropping it into the water.

Jonny had laughed affectionately, and they had continued their walk.

In the distance a small structure came into view, up ahead.

Before Jonny could work out what it was, Autumn screeched with delight and took off towards the building.

Confused, Jonny jogged after her.

When he stopped by the structure, he laughed aloud. It was a large playhouse, the size of a large shed, fully equipped with a little garden, a swing and stoop.

The stoop even had a small light that had illuminated when Autumn had excitedly pressed her face up against the glass window.

'Come on! We have to check this out!' she said, turning to him excitedly.

'What are you, six years old?' Jonny had said, laughing.

Then she pouted, walked over to him purposely, slowly and looked up into his eyes, seductively.

'Who knows? Maybe there's a mini bed in there?' she said with a lopsided grin.

'Yeah, you're right, we should get in, the weather could turn at any moment,' Jonny replied instantly, in mock seriousness.

Autumn laughed loudly, turned, and grabbed his hand behind her, leading him into the little house.

They both had to duck to enter. There was a light switch which Jonny pressed. It illuminated a cute, very pink, miniature cottage, complete with kitchen (fake appliances included), a fake fireplace and a couple of tiny seats, all pink.

To the right was a doorway which led to a tiny little bedroom with a window overlooking the grounds. There was a tiny bed in one corner with a bunch of blankets on it.

Jonny and Autumn looked at each other and laughed.

'Yeah, don't think my ass is going to fit on that, babe,' Jonny laughed.

'It will, but you'll bust it for sure, I bet my education on it,' she said back, giggling.

Autumn walked into the bedroom and Jonny followed. She took the blankets off the bed, arranging them on the floor next to it. The floor space was around the size of a double bed, which was perfect.

A single little light glowed from the ceiling, with another in the living area of the tiny house, illuminating very little.

Despite her warning, Jonny sat on the bed not thinking – it gave an audible groan, but held. He imitated wiping his brow in relief.

Autumn giggled, turned, and slowly began to unzip her gown. She held on to it and slowly turned to face him. She seductively, and ever so slowly, began to drop the gown.

Her shapely breasts popped out, standing proud.

Involuntarily, Jonny caught his breath in that moment. She looked incredible, as the moonlight shone through the window illuminating her, making her look almost ethereal. She really was an angel to him, and he loved her more than ever in that moment.

Autumn slipped the dress down to her hips and held it there, a smirk on her face, almost questioningly. Jonny sat with his mouth open, probably looking like the biggest of douche bags.

She played with the silky material, running it through one hand, then, to Jonny's delight, she suddenly pushed the gown and her dainty thong down in one. The garments fell, and landed softly around her feet.

He continued to stare, taking in her form. 'Absolute perfection' he thought to himself.

Her naked breasts heaved with the anticipation of what was to follow.

Jonny felt himself getting hard, a noticeable bulge in his

tux trousers, straining against the material, as if his manhood was trying to break out and escape.

Autumn noticed, and smiled innocently, feigning that she had no idea why this trouser malfunction was happening.

'Who's your friend?' she said with a laugh.

He sighed, laughed, and stood up. Unfortunately, Jonny had forgotten where he was, and smashed his head right into the roof.

'Bollocks!' He exclaimed, rubbing his head.

Autumn looked concerned for a split second, and then tried her best not to laugh, but it was no use. She burst out laughing, covering her mouth, tears welling in the corners of her eyes.

Jonny began to laugh then, and they both became almost hysterical.

'Thank God this isn't our first time... that really would have ruined it,' he said as their laughter's began to subside.

'Your friend still seems happy to see me, Jonny,' she giggled.

He looked down and laughed, then removed his tux trousers, followed by his shirt. He had no idea where his jacket was, somewhere in the main house no doubt.

Autumn stepped forward so that she was just inches from Jonny.

She placed her hand softly on his bare chest, and ran her hand down him, over his taught, youthful body, stopping at the top of his boxer shorts.

Suddenly surprising Jonny, Autumn yanked his boxers down to his feet in one quick swoop. His erection flew out, and he half expected a comical 'boing' noise as it stood hard and proud.

He looked at her again. He was almost salivating over

the beautiful sight before him. His loins were aching, as his manhood had grown to its absolute longest length.

Autumn kissed him, softly at first and then with more passion.

He fondled one of her pert breasts as the kisses became more urgent, passion building.

He stopped briefly to bend down and take one of her perfectly erect, pink nipples in his mouth. He licked and sucked it, running his tongue around the areolae. Autumn moaned in delight. He moved to her other breast and repeated his teasing, blowing on the now wet nipple, making her giggle and moan at the same time, as the cool air made it even harder.

She stepped away from him with a knowing grin, and slowly began to lower herself to the blankets on the floor.

She didn't lay down however, surprising Jonny. She dropped to her knees, ensuring her perfectly round ass stuck out in his direction.

Jonny didn't need to be told twice.

He kicked off his shoes and the bunched-up trousers and boxer shorts.

He bent down and softly touched the inside of one of her thighs, slowly working his hand up until he brushed against the small area of pubic hair that was delicately trimmed. With a slip of the thumb, he brushed against her soft, moist womanhood.

She gave an audible gasp as he moved his whole hand to cover her delicate, most private and sensitive of areas. He rubbed softly, in a circular motion.

He took her by surprise, bending down further and kissing her there, in the perfect spot. He felt the soft, delicate skin on his lips. He tasted her sweet elixir, making him almost delirious with lightheaded anticipation.

He ran his tongue up and down, moving faster and deeper until his tongue entered her.

She gave a squeal of delight, placing her hand behind his head, pulling him further, exciting them both to a whole new level.

Jonny couldn't take it any longer and it seemed, neither could Autumn.

He lifted his head, and in one smooth motion pushed himself inside her.

She gave a gasp, and practically screamed in pleasure. He started to rhythmically move his hips, thrusting into her, harder and faster.

He slowed for an instant to build up the tension and almost removed himself completely.

She made a moan that was almost a complaint. She pushed her head back and her hair brushed Jonny's hand that was placed lightly in the middle of her back.

He grabbed a huge handful of her dark, silky hair suddenly making her exclaim in excitement, 'Fuck yes!'

He thrust into her again, hard, and she yelled in ecstasy.

He continued to pump hard and fast, sweat dripping from his brow on to her back and buttocks, her back slick with sweat and passion also.

'Harder, deeper baby,' she screamed.

He gave her all he had to give, harder and even faster, incredibly deep, and the noise of their bodies slapping together was heaven. The ultimate elation. Every nerve in his body was alight with the pleasure and excitement.

They both knew the end was near and that climax was mercilessly inevitable.

They tried desperately to extend those last few moments,

and then they were both crying out together, as their juices were released in harmony.

Then, they both laid down, entwined in each other's bodies, naked and exposed, only to each other, the ethereal whisps of euphoria still lingering in the air.

CHAPTER 8

Jonny turned his gaze back to Autumn. He stared at her for a long time, as if he was trying to work out what to say.

He opened his mouth to begin to speak, stopped and closed it again.

Suddenly he blurted out: 'What happened, Autumn?'

She looked at him, a sad smile on her delicate features.

'I don't know yet, Jonny, honestly. I'll try to explain my best what's happening though, it will make it easier for you,' she said softly.

'I don't mean me, Autumn. Let's put a pin in me for a second as I don't even know if any of this is real. I could be dreaming, I could be high, shit I could have crashed into a tree down the road for all I know,' he said hotly, then continued almost in a whisper, 'Tell me... what happened to you that night, all I know is what they told me.'

He reached into his wallet and produced a folded, worn piece of paper. He opened it up and briefly looked at it before placing it on the table and turning it to face Autumn. It had pink flowers and unicorns patterned around the edges. She smiled sadly and said: 'You kept my note from that night.'

'Yeah, of course I did. I still can't believe Brad's little sister had paper and pencils in that playhouse!' he replied, smirking.

His smirk disappeared slowly, and he focused on her again. 'Please, Autumn... I need to know... what happened,' he pleaded.

She sighed, breathing in deeply as if she was preparing to dive into the ocean's dark abyss, which in a sense she was.

'As I wrote that note, I was heading to the house, as I needed to pee really badly and wanted to find my bag and check my phone,' she began.

'When I got up to the house, it was quiet. Everyone was asleep. People were laying everywhere, in all positions, it was almost funny. Brad had clearly fallen asleep early, as there were drawing of dicks, a moustache and a pirate's eye-patch on him.' She giggled at the memory and then became serious again.

'I found my bag near the front door, hanging with my coat where I had left it. I took it, found the bathroom and went for a pee. When I was finished, I washed my face and cleaned up my makeup in the mirror as best I could. Then I checked my phone. To my dismay, there were like twenty missed calls from my mum and five or six texts. I read them and my dismay turned into full-on panic. The gist was that my dad had woken in the night with chest pains and had got up to get a glass of water, waking my mum. He suddenly collapsed to the floor, unresponsive. Mum had called the emergency services, and in the last text she had said they were rushing to the hospital on blue lights and sirens. She said I needed to get there as soon as I picked up the message, as it didn't look good.'

She sighed and leant back into her seat. It was clearly difficult to relive this, Jonny thought. She stared at her hands and busied herself rubbing one of her nails.

'Then what happened, Autumn?' Jonny quizzed delicately.

She looked up, took another deep breath and continued.

'I tried to call my mum, but no answer and, as you know, I'm an only child so there was no one to help me. I called my cousin who I knew would be on his way there, but he didn't answer either.

'I tried both a few more times but had no luck. I threw my phone in frustration. I retrieved it and stuffed it into my bag, grabbed my coat and then went to Brad, who still hadn't moved from his spot on the sofa. I tried to gently wake him, but he wouldn't budge. I kicked him in frustration, and he sat up, bleary eyed and not very impressed. I said to him my dad might be dying and that I needed to get to the hospital right away. I said I needed to borrow his car, I begged him, and he reluctantly agreed and said the keys were in a bowl on the kitchen counter.

'I thanked him, ran to the kitchen, dug out the keys for his Mercedes and ran out of the front door. I found the convertible parked at the end of the drive, off to the side. I jumped in.

'I shot off down the drive and turned to get onto the main road.' Autumn hesitated, and tears began to well in her eyes.

Jonny placed his hand on top of hers. He smiled at her, trying to give her confidence to continue.

She nodded knowingly and continued: 'I know it was stupid, Jonny, but I had to get to my Daddy. If he had died, I would have never forgiven myself. I pushed the Mercedes hard. I flew down that country road, recklessly I admit it.' She choked back a sob as she continued the story.

'The alcohol had given me a flame in my stomach and resilience in my veins, so I pushed the car harder.

'I got onto a straight and floored it. In the distance I saw something, but by then it was too late, I was going too fast and was getting too close too quickly and I couldn't react... it was a damn badger!' she exclaimed in frustration.

'I swerved sharply, but I was going too fast. The rear of the car fishtailed, and I clipped the curb. It bounced off sideways, tyres screeching. Then the car flipped what felt like a million times in the air.

'The last thing I remember was the squeal of metal as my

side of the car smashed into something solid,' she said, tears now falling freely from her pretty eyes.

'It was a tree,' Jonny said delicately. 'I thought that was kind of what happened... the police and your parents filled in the rest. I suppose I just needed to hear it from you and know what happened,' he said to her reassuringly.

'I'm so sorry you had to experience that, Autumn, I truly am,' he said sincerely, whilst staring intently at her.

'Thank you,' she replied with a sniffle. She dabbed at her eyes with a napkin from the dispenser on the table.

'I'm sorry, Jonny,' she said suddenly, looking down at the now shredded napkin.

'I'm sorry I left you; I know that must have been really hard. We were so in love. I really think we would have been in it for the long haul,' she continued.

'You're right, babe. It was the hardest day of my life, and I've struggled since. It was a silly, reckless thing to do, Autumn, but it's not your fault, you need to know that,' he said to her firmly.

'Well, it doesn't look good on my record, does it?' she said looking at him oddly, as if she couldn't quite understand why he felt that way.

'I mean, why else do you think I'm here?' she continued.

'Here?' he questioned, sounding confused, 'What do you mean?'

Autumn looked equally confused and said again, 'Here...' as if it was obvious.

Then she continued, 'Here, as in Purgatory, Jonny.'

CHAPTER 9

Jonny laughed harshly. Autumn looked taken aback. She stared at him incredulously, with a hint of concern as someone who had just come across a lairy drunk would feel.

'I am bloody dreaming; I God damn knew it!' he said with a somewhat vicious smile.

Jonny gritted his teeth and stood suddenly. 'Fuck this,' he said forcefully.

He turned sharply and began to walk towards the entrance. It felt like an indefinite amount of time since he had entered the diner through that same door earlier.

'Where are you going?' Autumn called after him. She sounded like she was almost pleading with him. It made him stop and turn around. He surveyed his surroundings.

His eyes focused on an older man who sat in a booth on his own. He was looking at Jonny quizzically. He realized most people had turned and were looking at him in a similar way.

It had become noticeably quieter in the diner. Even the staff had stopped what they were doing and looked at him blankly.

Jonny focused again on the older man. He was dressed smartly in a three-piece suit. The clearly expensive suit looked like it was possibly turn of the century, early 1920s perhaps. His hair was brushed tightly to one side, clearly covering a bold spot, but was doing a good job, Jonny had to admit. He wore spectacles that perched on the end of his nose.

Jonny smirked and looked in Autumn's direction whilst shaking his head.

'That's how I know it's a damn dream,' he said with a jovial tone in his voice.

'I know my history,' he continued, 'and there is *no* way I would be in purgatory with actual royalty!' he almost shouted, pointing a stern finger at the older man.

Autumn didn't say anything at first. After a second passed, Jonny made a noise of disgust and turned. He began to stride towards the door purposefully.

'Stop!' Autumn shouted after him. 'Come back, let's talk, I'll explain everything Jonny!' she continued, her voice taking on an air of desperation.

Jonny got to the door and wrapped his palm around the handle tightly.

A cool breeze seemed to pass over him even though he stood under the door heater.

He didn't move. He stood, thoughtfully considering his situation. He realized there was now not a sound in the diner. It was silent. No noise from the kitchen, the jukebox had fell silent too... even the weather had died down to just a whisper of wind...the rain had subsided almost completely.

It was still dark as ink outside though, and as thick as the stuff too.

He turned his head one way and then another.

Everyone seemed to be subconsciously holding their breath.

Except one guy. He sat on one of the stools at the counter that surrounded the front of the kitchen. He was dressed in leather, clearly a biker. He had a long beard, handlebar moustache and a bandana holding back his long, mousy brown hair with hints of grey beginning to make their presence known. He was turned on the stool so that he could face the rest of the diner and survey the situation. He had one boot on the stool's footrest, the other on the floor, and his elbows leant on the bar counter behind him, lazily. He looked very relaxed, at home almost. He had a lop-sided grin and looked incredibly sure of himself.

He barked a laugh and pointed two fingers at Jonny, mimicking a pistol.

'I think you should go, buddy,' he stated simply and barked another laugh.

'DON'T listen to him, Jonny,' Autumn pleaded. She had begun to cry now, and Jonny's false bravado was beginning to wane.

'Yeah, go sit back down, Jonny, I'll bring you another shake, how about mint?' Ray said kindly from another table where he stood, previously serving.

'But... this is bullshit,' Jonny said to the room, his tone almost begging in the sense that someone would agree, that is bar the biker, of course.

The biker laughed, picked something from his tooth, which he unceremoniously flicked towards the jukebox and turned on his stool to face the kitchen again, clearly no longer interested.

'Jonathan,' Autumn said firmly.

Jonny's eyes snapped back to Autumn, his back now straight, making him almost stand to attention.

'Whatever,' he mumbled and began to slink back to his booth, like a scolded teenager.

He slid onto the bench in his booth.

Autumn stood a second longer, eyeballing him, then turning to stare daggers at the biker who was now engrossed in a bowl of God knows what soup, slurping it down loudly.

Autumn gave him one last burning stare and turned away, with a disgusted look on her pretty features.

She sighed, looked again at Jonny with an almost questioning look of 'are we good?' and then sat down heavily on the bench opposite Jonny.

Jonny looked down at the table and said nothing.

He slowly looked up and stared round the room.

In those few seconds, the diner had gone back to its normal and now familiar thrum of activity. The jukebox started a new track, something by Chris Stapleton he believed. Jonny was no Country and Western lover, on the contrary, but he *was* a fan of Chris Stapleton.

The murmur of countless conversations, all at once had also gone back to normal as had the diner's staff, rushing around, serving food, coffee and anything else the patrons required.

No one was looking in his direction either, everything was back to normal – even the damn weather had picked up its relentless howl again with the splattering of heavy rain drops against the panes of glass as if they were thousands of bugs hitting a windscreen during summer.

'I'm sorry,' he finally spoke. Autumn looked at him with a raised eyebrow and pointed to herself, as if she was saying 'Who, me?'. There was sarcasm behind this gesture and her look.

Her features softened then, and she quickly wiped away one last tear that had defiantly slid down her elegant cheekbone.

With that wipe, it seemed to figuratively wipe the slate clean also.

She sighed, relaxed back into the booth and said 'it's OK, Jonny. I understand. This is all a bit of a shock, I know, believe me'.

Jonny opened his mouth to reply, but before he could Ray appeared next to them, at the side of their booth and placed a big, green milkshake in front of Jonny. He placed a pink one in front of Autumn, grinning and gave her a wink. 'I know strawberry is your favourite, Autumn,' he said smiling kindly. She smiled back at him.

Ray turned to Jonny and his smile faltered slightly. He bent his knees so that he was around their head height. 'Thank you for not leaving, Jonny,' he said quietly, almost conspiratorially.

'Don't trust Bear over there,' he said pointing with his head. 'In fact, don't listen to anything he says,' Ray continued.

'Bear is a nasty piece of work, whose been here a while... it has felt like the longest time! He's a bit of a slimy guy, a grumpy old so and so too.' Ray said shaking his head slowly.

'He has done this before,' Autumn chimed in.

Jonny looked at Ray and then Autumn with a quizzical expression, he raised an eyebrow as if waiting for an answer.

Autumn obliged and said, 'He always tries to talk new people into leaving. Such a damn creep!'

Ray was nodding slowly in agreement.

'OK,' Jonny said flatly, looking at them both.

He placed both hands on the table, matter-of-factly.

'So, the guy's a complete dick hole, I get it,' he stated.

Autumn and Ray looked at each other and then back to Jonny and both nodded their agreement.

'That being said,' Jonny continued with a sigh. 'Why the hell do you guys care if I go outside? I just wanted to go for a smoke and clear my head. I probably would have come straight back in as the shitty weather would have put me off!' he questioned in a slightly animated voice.

Autumn and Ray looked at each other. Jonny could swear a look of concern passed on both their features before Autumn nodded and Ray responded.

'Look, Jonny,' he said with a tired sigh. 'This is Wendy's

job. She's the boss, but she's busy right now with another *new* customer,' he continued.

Autumn was focused on Jonny, but her eyes once flashed to Ray's, with a knowing look passing between them.

Before Jonny could speak, Autumn spoke. 'Wendy tells us the way of things here when we first arrive. She is kind of straight to the point, but she's a good woman and will explain everything.'

Ray picked up the conversation by stating, matter-of-factly 'Jonny. For now, Autumn will explain what she can...what she's allowed to.' He said this, with a quick, almost imperceptible turn of the head towards an unassuming looking door, next to the bathrooms, labelled, Private, Manager.

'I'll say one more thing before I go,' Ray continued. He took a deep breath before speaking again, as if he was psyching himself up to make the next statement, as that was what it was, a statement.

'Jonny, you can't go outside.'

'Yeah, I know, you guys have already said that,' Jonny replied tiredly with a roll of his eyes and a head shake.

'Let him finish!' Autumn said, almost in a hiss. She did not look pleased with Jonny's rebuke.

Patiently, Ray began again.

'Jonny. You. Cannot. Go. Outside,' he said firmly, drawing each word out as if they were an individual statement of their own. He clearly wanted to relay the importance of his words.

Before any other interruptions, Ray continued 'If you go outside, you can't come back'.

Ray looked at the door then, with a scared, haunting look in his eyes. He then said the last thing Jonny was expecting, and it scared him, to his absolute core.

'That door leads to Hell, Jonny.'

CHAPTER 10

Yet again, Jonny was lost for words. As he sat there, open mouthed, staring at Autumn and Ray, he had the insane temptation to laugh.

'This shit really just keeps getting crazier,' he thought to himself, a tired smile beginning to form at the corners of his mouth. The smile never reached his eyes though. His eyes were still sad, with the look of vulnerability and a childlike need for comfort.

He chastised himself internally, hushing the demons that continued to grow. He needed answers and he had a God damn million questions.

Before he could utter a single syllable though, the door at the back of the diner, marked Private and Manager flung open.

A scruffy looking teenager walked out, dragging her heels. She held a skateboard and her attire clearly showed that this was her chosen path in life.

She looked to be around sixteen and had the mood, posture and attitude that matched her age and looks perfectly.

'Can I help you?' she said rudely with great exaggeration and volume to an elderly couple (or who Jonny perceived were a couple) as she walked past them. They were sat in a booth closest to the bathrooms and the Manager's office.

They said nothing, looked away and continued playing some sort of card game, silently.

The girl turned and headed to one of the stools at the counter. When she turned, Jonny noticed she was not the only person to leave the back office.

A short, tired looking, slightly plump woman who must

have been in her early forties was following her, a fair few steps behind.

She had light, greying hair, cut to a bob and looked a little dishevelled as someone who had just worked a double night shift might.

Her shirt wasn't quite tucked into her trousers properly and the badge displaying the name Wendy was at an odd angle upon her chest.

As she walked, she ran a hand through her hair and rubbed one dark ringed hazel coloured eye.

She seemed to give herself a mental shake and stood straighter and almost marched, purposefully right towards Jonny, Autumn and Ray.

She slowed as she approached them and Ray skirted away quickly, not saying a word.

She stopped at the table and lay both hands upon it.

Jonny could see her close up now.

She looked older now and somewhat haggard. She clearly smoked, and a lot too.

When she spoke her voice was quite low, commanding but kind and raspy as someone's granny who smoked two packets a day.

'Jonny.' She said matter-of-factly. 'You're up,' she continued with a sigh, followed by a pause. 'When you're ready, follow me to the back,' she said and began to walk away before he could ask a single question.

As she walked, she said over her shoulder, 'Make sure you take a leak or whatever beforehand as this will take a while and I don't want to be disturbed once we get going.'

With that she walked through the office doorway, leaving the door ajar.

Jonny looked at Autumn, focusing on her elegant, soft

features. He seemed to himself that he was looking for clarity on what just took place.

She smiled at him and placed her hand on his. It was warm and gave him some confidence.

'Go,' she said simply with a smile.

'Wendy's a good person and will explain everything. I'll be right here waiting, don't worry. I'm not going anywhere, babe,' Autumn continued.

'OK, Autumn,' Jonny answered and slowly stood.

Jonny took a step and then on a whim, decided to bend down briefly and give Autumn a light kiss on the cheek. Her skin was warm and inviting and he felt better instantly.

He still had trepidation though as he began to walk stiffly towards the back of the diner.

As he approached the bathrooms and manager's office, he remembered what Wendy had said, and he decided to take a pitstop to urinate.

He changed his trajectory slightly and placed his palm against the men's bathroom door, ready to push it open.

He stopped though, mid opening.

He noticed the chef from the kitchen, a black man who looked around forty, walked out and headed purposefully towards the manager's office door, which was still ajar.

The man was big, really big. He must have been around six foot three or four and was big built, both muscle and fat it seemed.

Jonny estimated, looking at him, that he weighed in excess of 350lbs, perhaps 400lbs even.

He was sweating, and the hat above his hairnet had slipped so that it was at a comically jaunty angle.

Their eyes met briefly, Jonny gave the smallest of smiles in acknowledgment, but the cook ignored him and went into the office.

He did not close the door.

Jonny was about to walk through the men's bathroom doorway when he heard raised voices from the office.

'For fuck's sake, Frankie, how many times have I gotta tell you? Do I need to spell it out for you or something? Your shift ends when your shift ends! Simple. Same for me. Do I look like I want to be here? I am stressed to the eyeballs, overworked and I've got a pimple on my ass the size of a walnut that is killing me!'

Wendy all but bellowed at the man.

'Give me a break, Wend. Do you know how hot it is in that damn kitchen? To top it off, you send the little, mouthy, white bitch back out to wind me the fuck up! Ain't fair and you God damn know it!' Came the voice of the man who Jonny surmised was called Frankie from Wendy's earlier comment.

Before she could answer, Frankie was angrily shouting again. 'Lord knows I've done my time here and I deserve some rest bite. How about Janine gets her big ass in the kitchen instead, huh?'

There was a pause and then a quieter response that Jonny could not make out.

After that the conversation seemed to continue at that volume.

As Jonny could no longer decipher what was being said, he shrugged and walked into the men's bathroom.

The previous incident came to mind instantly, and he decided to head for the cubical instead.

He entered the dingy toilet stall and was unsurprised to find it fairly filthy. There were significant skid marks down the back of the toilet pan and paper in the bowl.

He averted his gaze in disgust and flushed the toilet.

He unbuttoned his jeans and did his business. He hadn't noticed how much he needed a piss after being cut off early last time.

As he continued to pee, he looked at the walls. They were covered with the usual graffiti, boogers and of course the obligatory glory hole, which as always in a public restroom, was stuffed with toilet paper.

The writings on the wall were the usual 'fucks' and 'shits' along with the 'Kim is a dirty whore' and 'Greg is a bumboy, call for a good time' followed by a phone number.

The difference though was that there were other writings on the wall that Jonny had not seen in a public bathroom before.

For example, there were odd symbols, prayers and dates. These dates sometimes had mini obituaries with them too. It was very odd and gave Jonny the chills.

He finished up and headed out. As he opened the door though he noticed one last comment that stuck out to him.

'Be careful. The Devil is amongst us' it read.

CHAPTER II

Jonny awoke to the noise of the terrible weather, the rain crashed down against the windowpanes, like tiny pebbles being thrown by invisible hands. The wind howled loudly, and the windows moaned, but there was another noise too.

The attic was making noises again, Jonny thought to himself, confused. A bang. A scuffle. Almost like someone or something was up there waiting for him.

He squeezed his eyes shut. Forcing himself to calm down. A tear slowly ran down his cheek.

He was shaking. But no matter what, he would not investigate...Jonny's eyes shot open, a look of complete bewilderment on his features.

'What the...' He said out loud and slowly looked around the dark room, dimly lit by the clouded moonlight outside. The curtains were wide open, and he knew it was a full moon, although barely visible, it hung there like forbidden fruit.

He could not believe it, he was back in his grandad's old house, in his bed, a small, helpless ten-year-old once again.

Another bang from the attic drew him from his reverie. He tried to ignore it but that same scratching noise from the attic began and quickly became persistent.

The noise became louder, more vigorous, more violent.

He squeezed his eyes shut again and didn't try to stop the tears that once again, freely ran down his cheeks, like the raindrops outside on the window.

'This cannot be happening' he thought to himself. He had dreamt this same dream countless times, but it *was* a dream, and he had known it!

This was different though. He could tell. He really was

there again.

Suddenly, all went silent.

No rain. No wind. No scratching from the attic. Nothing.

All he could hear was the quiet snores from his granddad's room.

No that's not true. That wasn't all he could hear.

He held his breath and listened hard. What was that?

It almost sounded like…whispering.

He slowly began to raise his head and look up at the ceiling, where the whispers were coming from.

As his eyes followed and looked up, in his peripheral vision he saw something move past the window.

He knew what was out there. He desperately did not want to look but knew he must. It was like rubbernecking at an accident…you don't want to look but you just can't help yourself. He slowly turned and stared at the window. The feeling of deja vu making his stomach lurch.

He could feel his heart thumping in his chest, like it was about to burst out his ribcage.

He let out a breath he hadn't noticed he'd been holding. A warm mist of air escaped his lips. The room had become freezing cold. Like ice. Like a morgue. He began to breathe lightly and quickly in a panic.

The more he breathed the more mist he saw expel from his lungs and mouth.

The whispers again. He shifted his gaze back to the ceiling. Scrutinising it, like it was about to come to life and open up, and let go of whatever misery was up there waiting for him. Watching him.

'Not again!' he moaned in barely a whisper.

As he knew there would be, outside behind the misty glass stood eight, maybe ten greyish white figures.

It was hard to see through the ever misting, wet panes of glass but there were many.

They all looked the same. No not the same, but similar. He couldn't make out their features as usual, but as always, they wore no clothes. They wore nothing.

The one closest to the window again seemed to have no feet. No legs. He looked down to the legs of an animal.

Jonny buried his head in his hands, knowing what would come next.

The lounge door flew open.

His grandfather stood in the doorway, in the shadows. Not moving a muscle.

He was petrified. He could not breathe. He stole looks between the abominations outside and his grandfather.

His grandfather slowly entered the room. Well, it seemed more like he floated in, glided almost, like a ghost would.

The dull light that seemed to be coming from the beings outside and the cloud covered moon, illuminated his grandfather pretty clearly.

Jonny choked out a cry. He tried to find his voice, but nothing would come out.

He was beyond petrified now; he thought he may go catatonic at this rate.

'What the fuck?' He finally managed to whisper in a shaking voice, that cracked at the end.

It was his grandad for sure, but he looked as if he had just come from the grave.

He was rotten, skin hanging off his bones, his eyes were missing, and his jaw hung broken, showing the mouth, open at an impossibly wide angle.

The smell that followed him made Jonny gag. The stench of decay and death.

His grandfather sat in his usual seat and faced the television once again.

There was no noise. You could hear a pin drop. He held his breath. More from terror than anything else.

Suddenly his grandfather's head snapped sharply right and stared at him through those dark empty eye sockets.

It was like staring into the entrance of hell, Jonny thought. Just then Autumn's face flashed into his mind, reminding him of the diner and the front door that apparently led to hell.

His grandfather then spoke. It was the same raspy voice as before, but Jonny could tell there were differences. It sounded dry like he had sawdust in his throat. The sound of death Jonny thought.

'Welcome,' the voice said. 'So, you are finally here.' There was a hint of arrogance and overall knowing to the voice that Jonny despised even more than the situation he found himself in.

'All you have to do now, is wake up and *leave that diner.*' His grandfather continued, in the alien voice.

'I'm not doing shit... why the hell should I... and why the fuck should I listen to you? You've been dead for three years!' Jonny spluttered, finding his voice finally. His voice sounded his own again, deep and familiar but scared shitless.

'Insolence!' the voice bellowed. Suddenly all the windows shattered outwards, and the wind and rain showered Jonny. Within seconds he was dripping wet and freezing cold.

'You know you must come with me. You know you deserve it. It is *your* fault that Autumn is dead, *yours* alone. Filthy little know-it-all you were and look what you and your disgusting genitals did... you killed her!' the voice continued, the wind howling around Jonny like a tornado. His grandad was unaffected by this; he just stared at him through those blank eye sockets.

The face was grinning now, and Jonny hated that more. It wasn't so much the nightmare of a monster that sat there staring at him, but the fact that it was still his grandfather. Why? Why did it have to be him. Let him rest in peace for God's sake!

The thing that resembled his grandad lifted a hand, palm up and stated, 'Need I say anymore?'

Jonny looked away. As much as he hated to admit it, this monster's words did have an effect on him. It was as if he knew Jonny's deepest darkest secrets... secrets and fears.

Jonny closed his eyes. Just for a second or two, trying to slow his breathing and not pop a gasket.

When he opened them, he was on the floor of the men's bathroom in the diner. He stared up at the blinking light over his head.

To the left of him, Ray was crouched staring at him with a concerned look, his eyes and features taught with worry.

'Jonny!' Ray said with relief, his whole body seeming to relax.

'Ray? What happened?' Jonny croaked.

He began to sit up and Ray helped him.

'I noticed you had been gone a while and as I needed a leak myself, I popped in and saw you lying here on the floor. I completely panicked and ran over to you, calling your name. A couple of seconds passed, and you awoke... and here we are', he said with a smile.

'Saying that,' he said looking at the cubical, 'I think I need to go in there now after finding you like that, I almost shat myself!' he said with a laugh.

Jonny laughed too and began to stand.

'Ohh let me help you,' Ray said, concern etched in his

voice once again.

Jonny allowed Ray to assist him stand. He then went to the sink and washed his face and hands.

'What is going on in this place Ray... is this normal?' Jonny questioned, looking at Ray in the mirror.

Ray shuffled awkwardly, averting his gaze and said quietly 'I don't think it is normal Jonny... but it's not for me to say... Wendy will explain, I'm sure.'

'Sure. No worries,' Jonny said. 'Thank you, Ray, you're a good guy to have around,' he continued with a tired smile.

With that, Jonny headed for the exit whilst Ray went into the cubical and closed the door.

Jonny turned and was about to enter the back office when Wendy appeared, her arms folded across her breasts. She did not look happy.

'What happened? You fall in?' she questioned matter-of-factly.

'Sorry,' Jonny mumbled. 'I passed out and had a flashback to when I was a kid... Ray found me on the floor and helped me,' he continued.

Her hard stare changed for a split second. It was one of pity and...was that fear?

Before Jonny could say anything else, her usual hardened look reappeared and she said, 'Come on, I haven't got forever.' With that she turned and headed into the office.

'Don't sugar coat it,' Jonny mumbled to himself, and walked into the manager's office, closing the door behind him.

CHAPTER 12

Jonny clutched his stomach, bending over in sickening fright as he looked around the office.

He looked down and it felt like all his insides did a summersault.

It was endless, office after office, all exactly the same looking, as far as the eye could see.

Down, left, right, up and insanely, behind him too. There must have been hundreds, maybe thousands, even millions!

He grabbed the door handle behind him, preparing to leave, a look of pure terror was stuck to his features, like some B grade horror movie.

'Opps! Sorry, Jonny, I should have warned you about that,' Wendy said tiredly, seeming to be not overly concerned.

She was already seated behind the large wooden desk in the centre of the room. She was concentrating on a file that lay open in front of her.

'Frigging, Frankie.' She muttered, shaking her head. 'If he hadn't put me off with his bullshit, I would have remembered,' she continued.

She looked up then and gave him a tired smile, a look of empathy crossing her features.

'Sorry again, truly. Ignore all that and come take a seat. It's all perfectly safe I promise you, plus over here there's a big round rug under the desk, so you don't have to look down,' she said pointing below the desk.

Jonny let go of the door handle, having to mentally pry his hands from the knob.

He slowly begun to walk towards Wendy's desk and the proffered seat.

Jonny stopped when Wendy did a sort of snorting laugh and choke at the same time. She coughed then, long and hard. She shook her head with a grin that she clearly was trying to hide.

'Sorry. You just... you look like a damn deer on ice!' she said, placing her hand on her forehead.

She shook her head with a grin and looked down again at the file. She then began to type on a comically looking old keyboard, connected to an archaic looking computer.

Jonny finally made it to the seat, reaching out to grab it for support.

He quickly sat and sighed with relief, expelling a long slow breath that he hadn't realised he had been holding.

'Smoke?' Wendy asked, offering a pack of cigarettes.

'Yes please, thank God!' Jonny said both hands raised up to the air whilst he looked up. He regretted this however as all he could see again were countless offices, just like the one he was sat in.

An almost unbelievably huge woman looked down at him from above. She was sat in the same seat as him, but one story up of course.

She was so large that only one buttock seemed to fit on the seat.

Jonny had what he thought, was a rational fear that she might end up on top of him, and if that happened, he had no chance!

She stared for a few seconds longer, her double...or was it triple chin, grotesquely squashed against her non-existent neck... or that Jonny could tell anyway. She had only a blank expression on her features.

When she looked away, Jonny noticed a small cylindrical item beside her on wheels. It was an oxygen tank he realised.

The woman was so huge that she needed assistance breathing, he guessed.

'Listen. I know I said you're completely safe, hun, but if that big girl farts, we are both gonna be blown into particles floating in space forever!' Wendy said with a laugh, shaking the cigarette pack at Jonny that she was still holding.

He took one and placed it between his lips, smiling. Wendy lent over and lit the cigarette for Jonny; he inhaled deeply. He blew a long stream of blue smoke, instantly feeling a little bit calmer.

Suddenly, it occurred to him that they should not be smoking inside, it was against the law.

With concern in his voice, he asked Wendy, 'Hey, are we OK to smoke in here... it's against the law, no?'

She silently laughed, whilst placing her own cigarette between her lips and lighting it.

As she blew a cloud of smoke out, sharply to the left and with a lop-sided grin she said, 'Things are a little different here, hun... hence the otherworldly structure your currently sat in.'

Jonny shrugged his shoulders in a sign of acceptance and continued to enjoy his cigarette. He noticed an ashtray on the table and flicked some into it.

It was a tacky holiday souvenir, a picture of Niagara Falls stared up at him, covered in ash.

'Another life,' she said almost amused, noticing Jonny studying the ashtray.

Jonny felt a little more settled now, if that was possible, he mused. He took in his surroundings. There was a fairly plain looking door at the back left of the office, that led God knows where, he thought. There was a grey, rusty old filing cabinet against the right glass wall, with a lamp on top of it.

He turned in his chair to look behind him, the way he had come. The closed door sat there, looking no different than any other door. It had a frosted circular window near the top. Jonny wondered if you could make out anything on the other side if you pressed your nose right up against the glass. Would it be the next office, or crazily, the diner? He shook his head, knowing this was not helping anything.

Wendy clearly noticed his child like wonder, whilst he observed the room.

'Don't let things like that confuse you for now,' she said pointing towards the doorway he had walked through, less than five minutes ago. 'Let's just focus for now, we will circle round to all that later, OK?' Wendy said quickly.

'Right,' she said slapping the file in front of her, changing the subject. 'Let's get started.'

Before Wendy could say another word, the plain door behind Wendy, in the far-left corner of the office opened swiftly.

An impossibly tall man entered, he looked as tired as Wendy but wired as if he had been up all-night doing speed.

Jonny looked at him in surprise. Further surprise crossed his features as he looked behind the man into the corridor that was now visible behind him. It was impossibly long, and he could see door after door on one side…he guessed it was mirrored on the other side of the corridor also.

He was so confused. Everything was glass here… he could see everything! So, where the hell was this corridor? He looked into the office directly in front of him that was currently void of anyone.

There was a door at the back there too, but it was closed currently. The door at the front of the office, was much like the front door in this room, down to the circular frosted window. Jonny wondered where that led, to the diner, or somewhere else?

He continued to look at the empty office. What happened when you opened the frosted windowed door in that office – would it open in this office too? He was so confused... all this glass!

Just then, the door in question *did* open, to his utter surprise. There was no sound from that office and it only opened within that room.

Suddenly a small, long-haired man appeared in the doorway, in that office, directly across from Jonny's. He seemed to be wearing a grey suit, the trousers too baggy. He was carrying a mug of something.

Jonny's mouth fell open. The man had literally appeared out of thin air!

'This place is a mind fuck,' he stated more to himself than anyone else.

Wendy and the crazily tall man both looked at him, Wendy grinning. He hadn't realised he was talking out loud. 'I'm going nuts,' he told himself mentally.

'Bob, I am in a meeting here. Can't this wait?' Wendy chided the tall man.

'Forgive me, Wendy, but your latch was green, so I came right in,' the tall man, apparently called Bob, said.

Jonny looked at the door and noticed Wendy stretching to look at it also.

Jonny could clearly see a small panel with a slider at eye level on the back of the open door. It was green and he guessed, if you slid it the other way, it would show red.

'Give me a break!' Wendy said irritably.

'Jonny, I am so sorry about this. It's not getting off to a good start hey?' Wendy said turning to Jonny. A sad smile on her face.

'What is it Bob,' she asked with a sigh, not even turning to look at the tall man.

Bob looked from Wendy to Jonny, an apologetic smile on his elongated features.

He wore a suit minus the jacket. His waistcoat was unbuttoned, and he had a lanyard around his neck. A card was attached to it, but Jonny couldn't make out anything on it, he noticed curiously.

He was bald and seemed to be in his fifties perhaps, he was of average appearance with nothing standing out apart from his sharp grey green eyes and thick rimmed glasses.

'It's been confirmed for this sector,' he said to Wendy, conspiratorially. It was just louder than a whisper, but Jonny could hear the comment clear enough in the near silent room.

Wendy looked away and muttered something under her breath... Jonny guessed she was cursing again.

'OK, thank you, Bob,' she said turning back to the tall man.

'I'll be on the lookout; I'll give you a ring if anything comes up,' she continued.

Bob looked like he wanted to say more. He nervously looked at Jonny and then back to Wendy. 'OK then,' he said simply, placing what Jonny guessed was a false smile, for his benefit, across his features.

He did a little wave, turned, and walked out the room, closing the door behind him.

There was definitely no corridor behind that door that Jonny could see now, he mused.

All he could see was the next office, behind theirs.

Suddenly, Bob appeared in that office too, through the door at the back left corner. The bold man that Jonny had seen walk in a few minutes ago, was now seated behind the desk. He peered up at Bob, he had clearly been engrossed in the paperwork on his desk.

Jonny watched as they silently spoke, no noise passing between the glass panels of the offices.

There was no one else in that office… but then… he noticed a boy in the corner of that room, looking down into another office. Jonny hadn't noticed him before, probably because he was sat on the floor.

He must have been only eight maybe nine… his sandy hair was flopped over his face, disguising his features. He wore shorts and an orange t-shirt.

'Jesus!' Jonny exclaimed. 'Children, really?' he said focusing on Wendy, his tone accusatory.

She raised her eyes from the file in front of her and turned slowly to look at the boy. She turned back and continued to look at the file, clearly not bothered.

As she looked down, she picked up a pen and began to make notes.

As she did this she spoke. 'All shapes and sizes here, buddy,' she said in a jovial tone.

Jonny stared at her open mouthed, and then simply shook his head.

'This damn place,' he said quietly to himself.

'If I was you, I would focus on myself right now, yeah?' Wendy said curtly, looking at him with frustration in her eyes.

'My patience is wearing thin, Jonny. It's been a crap day, and I don't need any heroes, OK? You wanna talk about you or a boy who thought it was OK to push his sister into the cedar rapids, whilst full well knowing she couldn't swim, just to get his mum's attention?' she said forcefully.

'He killed her?' Jonny asked, shock ebbed over his features.

'Yeah,' Wendy said with a 'well duh' look on her face.

'But he didn't do it to kill her, therefore not on purpose... that's why he's here like the rest of you,' she continued.

'Now. On to you,' she said, again looking at the file, the previous conversation clearly over.

'So... you killed a man,' she said plainly, not even looking up.

Jonny looked down in shame, and with a barely audible voice, said 'Yes.'

CHAPTER 13

Jonny had struggled through university after Autumn had passed.

As she was not there to join him, it never felt right. Brad had begun to drift away from him after starting university too. They were still friends, but it was a somewhat strained relationship as is such when something terrible happens.

Jonny ended up being somewhat of a loner for the first six months.

After this, the university therapist had suggested he reconsider his options regarding the courses he was taking.

He did as she suggested and decided to do a complete U-turn and changed his major to photography.

He loved photography, especially taking scenic shots of forests. There was something magical about the huge trees with that intoxicating woody, earthy odour.

Since Autumn had passed, he had found himself hiking more often, in search of a sanctuary which usually ended up being a forest.

The sound of the trees brushing together in a light breeze, the soft moss-covered ground and the sound of wildlife really did make it a place he could relax. It was the only type of place where he felt he could switch his brain off, even if it was just for a few hours.

Sometimes he would visit a forest that had a water source, a lake or perhaps even a waterfall. This just added to the enchanting feeling he would feel within his soul when visiting, somewhere so private and personal.

This passion in woodland and photography had seemed the perfect idea to change his major to photography.

Autumn had loved taking photos too and he had on more than one occasion snapped some epic photos of her, according to Autumn.

She had said he had 'the eye' for it and because of that it sealed his decision to change.

After university, Jonny had been lucky. The first job he had applied for had accepted him. It was a small photography firm that were booked to do landscape photography for a number of country magazines and the like.

Jonny had quickly shown his talent, and the Managing Director had noticed this. He had taken him under his wing and helped him become a truly talented photographer.

A couple years in and not only did he have the qualifications, but he also now had the real-world experience to match.

Jonny had been seconded in his third year with the company to an American organisation, that their company had a joint venture with, over in the States.

They had wanted the British company's best photographer, so the MD had offered it to Jonny.

With no real ties, he had jumped at the opportunity.

In less than eight weeks, he had jumped on a plane with his most prized possessions, and flown to Montana, where he would be based.

It had been an epic experience. He was there just over eight months and loved every minute of it. He even met a girl there, a nice American girl that was homely, warm and loving.

He had managed to put Autumn to the back of his mind during this time.

Life seemed to be on the up but as always with these peaks, there are usually troughs also.

His friend and mentor, Gary, the Managing Director of the company suddenly passed away from a heart attack.

Jonny was beside himself over this and flew back to the UK as quickly as possible.

Once he had attended the Funeral, the board asked him to come in for a meeting at their office in Bristol.

Jonny lived near the coast, on the border between Devon and Somerset so he was not a massive distance from the office. Before the secondment he visited the office weekly in fact.

The thought of Gary not being there though saddened him, and he really didn't know if he was up to making the trip, just after the funeral.

He knew he had to though, and so he made his way by train.

Jonny assumed that after Gary's passing, the board would decide to make some changes such as changing roles and cancelling his secondment. The work had been good and strong in the States, but he knew the board were divided on this project as it had initially only been planned for six months.

It turned out Jonny was right regarding the secondment. They wanted him back in the UK. But not for the reasons he had expected.

Jonny had sat in the main meeting room in the office, the six board members all looking at him in anticipation.

He couldn't believe it. They wanted him to take Gary's role as Managing Director. The only difference would be that this was a hybrid role. He would be expected to be in the office twice a week, one day at home and two days out on the road, still doing actual photography.

He had not known what to say. As they continued to stare at him in anticipation, he had felt forced to make a decision then and there, which he was not comfortable with.

He had asked for some time to think it over, just that morning even.

They had reluctantly agreed, and Jonny had left the office to go for a walk and get some fresh air.

He returned after lunch. He had spoken with his mum, and they had talked through the situation. She had made him realise there really were not many reasons to say no.

The pay would triple for one thing, and the other benefits were very good also.

'What about Sammy?' he remembered asking her.

'If she is *the one*, she will follow you my love,' his mother had replied.

Jonny had accepted the role that afternoon. He was still slightly undecided but felt he had made the right call, and he knew that was what Gary would have wanted.

It turned out Sammy was not '*the one*'. She had been excited for him when he told her, but when he explained he had to stay in the UK, she had become upset. She had never left the States and although she agreed she would like to visit; she had no plans to live anywhere else.

Sammy was a few years younger than Jonny, and Jonny couldn't blame her for wanting to find her feet in this world.

Soon after, they had agreed to stay in touch, but just as friends as this clearly wasn't going to be viable as a relationship any longer.

Jonny moved closer to the office that summer. He purchased a brand new, large, detached home on the outskirts, where Somerset boarded Bristol.

It was a lovely, quiet area. A small development of exclusive homes that made Jonny feel he had accomplished something.

Shortly after moving in, he decided it was time to grow up and sell his little sports car. It was showing its age anyway.

Jonny always liked to be a little different and with his fondness for America, he had stopped at the local Jeep dealership one day after work, on his way home.

Jonny walked out ninety minutes later, having just placed his order for a brand new Grand Cherokee Summit edition.

He had ordered it in Deep Auburn, an unusual brown/bronze colour. In this spec, it came with a chocolate brown interior that he was told was extremely rare and would help with its residual value.

After this, he settled into his new role as Managing Director and surprised himself with how much he enjoyed it.

It was hard and more work for sure, but he did well, and the board noticed this, giving him a pay rise, just three months in.

Shortly after this he got a phone call from Jeep confirming his SUV would be ready for collection that Saturday.

That morning, he had left his house with his father in toe, excited.

He had never purchased a brand-new vehicle, and this was special to him.

Although slightly extravagant, Jonny had convinced himself it was much better value than buying a Range Rover and he needed a four-wheel drive. The finance wasn't too pricey, and, on his salary, he felt he would hardly notice the payments each month.

Turning up and seeing that big hulking beast sat in the dealership under a cloak had made his insides tingle with anticipation.

When they had pulled the sheet off, theatrically, he had been giddy with joy.

The paintwork shone like a new penny under the dealership lights; it twinkled at him like it had millions of little stars imbedded in the paintwork. This was thanks to the pearlescent coat and colour choice, he thought.

After completing the paperwork and handing over the keys to his old car, Jonny and his dad had jumped in the Jeep and got on the open road.

They opened the panoramic roof, blasted the stereo and enjoyed the sunny weather – the wind tousling their hair.

They had decided to go the scenic route back to Jonny's house. For a long while they went in the complete wrong direction, not by mistake but just so they could enjoy the drive. A bit of father and son time too.

They approached a village and Jonny decided to stop to fill up the Jeep as it only had a quarter of a tank of fuel to start with and that was now even less.

The Jeep had a large fuel tank, so he stood for quite some time at the pump, just filling.

A shabby looking van had pulled up behind them, just after Jonny had got out the car.

Unfortunately, there were only two pumps at this village fuel station, and the other was out of order.

Jonny briefly made eye contact with the man behind the wheel of the shabby looking van.

He stared daggers back at him.

Jonny looked away. 'Someone's having a bad day,' he thought.

Suddenly the driver began to honk the van's horn.

Jonny looked over frowning.

His dad got out the passenger side and looked over at the van's single occupant.

He cheerfully said aloud, 'Not long sorry! Nearly done.'

Jonny was surprised then when the man stepped out of the van, his big beefy head bright red with anger.

'By then there won't be any fucking diesel left will there?' he shouted at them both. 'You've had your fill now move your fancy new car off the lot!' He continued, angrily.

'Calm down, buddy, we are just finishing up,' Jonny's Dad replied, a little more firmly, his jovial tone now completely gone.

To Jonny's further surprise the man marched up to his dad, nose to nose and squared up to him.

Jonny's dad was ex-military, so he wasn't going to take any bullying. The man had his finger in Jonny's dad's face.

Jonny's dad grabbed his finger and shoved him slightly, yet firmly in a way to warn him to back off.

The oaf of a man didn't get the hint though.

Jonny's dad was in great shape for someone in their late fifties. This guy looked around forty, unkept and overweight. His belly hung over his jeans which were smeared with oil stains.

His vest had not come off any better it seemed.

To both their surprises, the man rushed Jonny's dad and head butted him!

Jonny couldn't believe it. He leapt into action, running round the side of the truck to confront the man.

His dad's nose was bleeding, and he had his hand to his face.

The man was shouting saying things like, 'what you gonna do now old man,' and 'I warned you!' He didn't see Jonny approach.

Jonny shoved him hard from behind, the man stumbled but maintained his footing.

He whirled on Jonny and went to punch him in the face. Jonny had already foreseen this coming however, so he had moved to one side slightly. The glancing blow on his shoulder had not hurt but enough was enough.

Jonny pulled his arm back, strong muscles quivering, and shot a right hook right in the guy's face.

He had looked shocked. In slow motion he stumbled backwards, and the back of his head cracked on the petrol pump's corner.

Blood erupted everywhere. The guy was out cold.

Jonny had looked at his dad, both had concern on their faces.

Just then someone rushed out from the petrol station and asked what was going on. The witness said they had seen the man try to attack Jonny and his father, but nothing else.

Jonny had confirmed this and then explained quickly that he had hit him back in self-defence.

The man had accepted this and had ran back inside to call an ambulance as the large man on the floor was still unconscious and could not be shaken awake.

His dad had cared for him there, tried to support his neck and stem the bleeding.

The ambulance had turned up ten minutes later followed by a police car.

The police had taken a statement off both Jonny and his dad whilst the man was being treated in the ambulance.

Another police officer had taken a statement from the forecourt attendant also.

Just as they were closing the ambulance doors, they all watched in horror as the paramedics tried to hold the large man down; he was having a seizure.

Jonny then heard the dreaded noise that still haunts him to this day. A heart monitor making a perpetual dull alarm noise.

The man had died.

CHAPTER 14

The trial had not lasted long. In the grand scheme of things, it was a fairly low-key incident with very little interest.

The jury had decided it was indeed self-defence, and it could not have possibly been known, by Jonny, that a punch would have killed the man.

The prosecution tried to argue that Jonny knew his own strength and should have simply tackled the man rather than punch him.

They sealed their own fate with this though as it showed they clearly knew the man was unhinged and baying for blood at the time.

Just like the jury, even the prosecution could not deny that it was self-defence from that statement.

Jonny was acquitted and very little follow up bothered him after this – even the man's family – the ones still in touch with him that was – did not seem overly pushy towards trying to get Jonny wrongly put away.

His career on the other hand did suffer. The board were nervous around the incident and how it would affect them and the company – Jonny too, did not feel himself after this and made the quick decision that he would leave.

Before he could give his notice however, he was paid off to leave quietly.

It was a large pay off, so Jonny cleared all his debts, the house, the car and a couple of credit cards.

He then sold the house he had come to fondly call home and moved back down to the very South of Somerset, again kissing the boarder of Devon.

In an old, converted barn, he set up home, once again. It

was quiet, rural and had just two neighbours, both a couple hundred feet away. Bar this, there was no one for miles.

All that he could see from the huge barn doors on the south side of the barn, was green hills, forests and nature.

It instilled a sense of calm in him.

Shortly after moving in, he had a conservatory fitted to the south side of the barn so he could enjoy the sun setting, surveying his couple of acres of Paradise.

Now, when you stepped from the big old barn doors, you were not greeted with mud but with warm slate tiles in the conservatory.

He put beds in on each side of the long, slim conservatory so that it almost felt like he was bringing the outside in.

On the mezzanine balcony, that sprawled out over half the barn, he set up his office, right next to the master bedroom.

All his equipment was neatly put in its place, and he got right into setting himself up as a freelance photographer.

The incident thankfully did not really follow him, and he found work quickly, that was well paid and enjoyable.

Thanks to not having any debt now or money worries, Jonny found he could work for the pure enjoyment of photography now. This was in contrast to the rather half and half which he had become accustomed to in the city.

Quite a bit of Jonny's work was now in editing. He was emailed projects to work his magic on, he was still paid the same and enjoyed creating a beautiful picture, a one-off masterpiece.

Jonny struggled to sleep though, even in this serene setting, the raindrops lightly pattering against the Velux window above his head at night, he could not settle.

He would think again and again about what happened with his father that day. He would also think about Autumn a lot. His thoughts of Sammy were rare; it always ended up being Autumn.

It was her soft smile and delicate features that he would see in his mind's eye as he slowly drifted off into a fitful sleep.

The barn was long and in the main living area, the ceiling was the roof itself. It stretched up incredibly high.

With a roaring fire in the log burner, which sat snug within the huge fireplace, Jonny would stare up at the ceiling, fascinated by the huge, varnished trusses that held the massive structure up.

They were a beautiful dark ocean blue, as was the rest of the woodwork in the house. It was one of the things that stood out to him on his first viewing, and it definitely helped sell the property to him.

Next door was an open barn full of hay, wood and old bits and bobs left by the previous owners. At the very end of the structure, slightly down hill was a workshop. This workshop was two stories and was a bit of a mess. It was covered in dust and seemed to have not been used in some time.

Jonny had done nothing with this as of yet, he had just stored some suitcases in there, that was it.

One windy night in April, Jonny had gone out the front door to get some ice out of the chest freezer, which was located in the open barn, all be it protected with a wooden side wall, from the elements.

Jonny had got ice and slipped it into his tumbler which was half full with a generous shot of whiskey.

As he began to head back towards the front door of the barn, he noticed something odd.

A light was on in the workshop at the bottom of the property.

He looked at it for a moment, confused.

He shrugged his shoulders and began to walk back, to the main barn.

He got in and closed the door behind him. Before he kicked off his shoes however, curiosity got the better of him and he slipped on his heavy winter coat, and trudged back outside, closing the door behind him.

He headed down the soft hill, past the open barn and to the very end where the workshop was.

The light was still on, and he swore he saw a figure pass across the window.

Jonny ducked in fear of being seen.

He grabbed the closest thing next to him to potentially use as a weapon.

It was an axe, which he used to cut up firewood.

He slowly walked to the door, crouching so that he would not be seen through the window.

Before he could talk himself out of it, he grabbed the handle and burst in.

Sitting on the floor, on a dirty old picnic blanket was a girl, perhaps eighteen years old.

She twisted round in shock and then stood up, fear in her eyes, her hands raised up in a gesture of surrender.

'Hey, easy, dude,' she said quickly. 'I was just looking for somewhere to crash for the night and the door was unlocked. I got lost on a hike through the hills and found your barn,' she continued, sounding somewhat panicked.

Jonny's fear and anxiety ebbed slightly, and he lowered the axe.

'Why didn't you just knock on the door, I could have helped,' he questioned her.

'Dude, I'm a nineteen-year-old girl, I weigh like 115lbs, who am I gonna take on if someone decides they want to go all 'Buffalo Bill' on me?' she said with a smirk.

Jonny couldn't help but laugh at this. 'Hey, you're right, I get it,' he said with a kind smile.

'Look, its bloody freezing tonight, I've got the log burner going at full chat in there, why don't you come in, warm yourself and kip on the sofa for tonight?' he said to her putting the axe down.

Before she could answer, he added, 'I won't chuck you down a well or nothing, I swear!'

She laughed at the movie reference and scratched her neck, thoughtfully.

She seemed to make her mind up then and there on the spot suddenly. 'Screw it. If you were gonna kill me, I'd be dead by now. Lead the way maestro,' she said, smiling.

Within an hour, Jonny had learned that the strange young woman sat next to him on his couch in front of the fire, was called Hattie. She didn't have a permanent residence as such, and instead enjoyed moving around, place to place with friends in campers going to festivals and events.

She seemed to strongly resemble a hippy with her colourful clothes, big woolly hat and multitude of piercings.

She removed her hat after some time and shook her long blond hair out. It was a dirty blond colour and had purple highlights at the very front. She had piercing blue eyes and Jonny thought to himself that she would be quite pretty if not for the baggy clothes and unkept look – but hey, who was he to judge? She could do what she liked.

Living off the land, (effectively) definitely had its charm about it.

They chatted well into the night, enjoying each other's company. They drank, ate some cheese and biscuits and discussed many subjects.

Hattie had an interesting perspective on many things including life.

Jonny felt almost envious of her free spirit and way of thinking.

When it was extremely late, or extremely early, depending on how one would look at it, he decided it was time for bed.

Hattie had said she was beet too. He grabbed a couple of blankets and a spare pillow and said she was welcome to a spare bedroom on this, the ground floor.

She decided instead to opt for staying on the sofa, where it was still warm, even with the dying embers of the once roaring fire.

Jonny awoke a few hours later. It was not yet dawn, but it was getting there.

For an instant, he couldn't work out why he had been awoken.

That was until he saw the form of Hattie stood at the end of his bed.

She was naked, bar one of the blankets he had given her, which was draped around her shoulders and head.

She was shivering. 'S... sorry Jonny,' she mumbled through chattering teeth. 'I don't feel so good,' she continued.

Jonny sat up sharply and flicked on the bedside lamp.

Her skin was extremely pale with a hint of grey to it. Her eyes were like saucers, there was no colour there hardly, just the unnaturally huge pupils.

She did not seem to care about her nakedness, or perhaps she didn't even notice.

Jonny quickly realised she was high.

Alarmed, he got up and settled her on the bed.

He crouched down so that he was eye level with her. Her breasts protruded from under the blanket. He only looked for a fleeting second and then chided himself; 'knock it off, she needs help, you prick'.

He reached out a hand and pulled the blanket tighter around her body to cover her modesty.

'Hattie. What have you taken?' he said, quietly yet firmly.

She looked away, not wanting to answer, almost embarrassed.

'Hattie?' he questioned in a voice not dissimilar to the way one would chide a puppy for ripping up the Sunday paper.

'Just a little smack I had left over,' she said apologetically.

Before he could say anything else she continued, 'I'm sorry, Jonny, I shouldn't have brought it into your home, I just wanted a little pick me up to help me sleep is all!' Her voice was somewhat desperate, even pleading.

'Hattie, that stuff will kill you,' Jonny warned.

She ignored the comment and said, 'Can I stay, Jonny? You seem a nice guy and I just want somewhere to stay for a while, even just a few more nights?'

'I'm sorry, Hattie,' Jonny said standing and crossing his arms.

'You can't stay any longer, when its light you'll have to leave,' he continued firmly.

She looked sad and began to fiddle with a loose thread on the blanket.

She stood then, slowly but still surprising Jonny.

She purposefully slipped the blanket off her shoulders revealing her naked body.

She was young, taught and firm breasted, Jonny noticed. He couldn't help but look.

The mound of unkept hair above her womanhood was the same dyed purple. A tattoo of a snake slithering out from one side to the other would have made Jonny smile in any other situation.

'I'll fuck you,' she stated matter-of-factly. 'I'm a filthy girl,' she continued, slowly approaching him. 'Let me stay Jonny, bung me a couple of notes to help me out and I'll make every night the best of your life,' she said with a forced smile.

With a sad smile, Jonny looked at her and placed a hand on her shoulder.

'I'm sorry, Hattie.' Was all he said.

He picked up the blanket, draped it around her body and walked her out to the mezzanine office and down the quirky stairs to the living area.

Once Hattie had realised her allure was not going to work on Jonny, she began to pack her few belongings and sadly smiled at Jonny.

She had calmed down now, both from the odd incident upstairs but also from the drugs in her system.

At the front door, she randomly hugged Jonny tightly and thanked him for letting her stay.

'Please, Jonny,' she said one last time, pleadingly as the sun broke through the clouds showing that morning had truly broken.

'I am sorry, Hattie; I wish you the best,' Jonny said with a sad smile. He slowly closed the door, Hattie still standing there, a pleading look on her features.

When Jonny returned to the front door a few minutes later, she had gone.

He checked the rest of his property, and she was nowhere to be found.

A couple of days later, Jonny went out in the Jeep to get some much-needed shopping from the local village shop that was four or five miles away.

On his way up the ridiculously steep hill that left the three properties, including his own, at the bottom of the valley he noticed a vehicle, parked right by the gate that led out on to the fast country road.

As he got closer, he noticed it was a police car.

A police officer got out and waved for him to stop.

He did so and put the Jeep in park. The police officer walked to the driver's side of the car and spoke to Jonny through the open window.

'Morning, sir,' the officer spoke professionally, but his smile was kind.

'Hi. Anything I can help with?' Jonny said to him.

'No, we are nearly done here, you'll just have to wait fifteen or twenty minutes and then you can get past,' he stated politely.

Before Jonny could say anything in reply, the police officer asked him a question with a quizzical look in his eyes, 'Have you seen anyone round here in the last couple of days that shouldn't have been here sir?'

Jonny didn't want any trouble and stupidly answered, all to quickly 'No, quiet as normal, just me and my photography.'

The police officer looked thoughtful and then said, 'OK, no problem. I'll give you a shout when you can go forward, I'll move the police car shortly.'

'Sorry, officer,' Jonny said before the police officer could return to his vehicle. 'What has happened here, if you don't mind me asking?' he continued.

The officer was quiet for a second, seeming to internally weigh up if he should say something or not.

With his mind clearly made up he said quietly, 'We found a girl this morning, right by the gate there in the bushes. A hippy kind of girl, dirty blond hair with purple streaks. Looks like she was a drug user, there's a needle in her arm,' he said sadly.

'Was?' questioned Jonny.

'Yeah,' the police officer said, pausing.

'She's... dead, I'm afraid.'

CHAPTER 15

'You still with me, champ?' The words brought Jonny quickly back to earth... or wherever this was.

'Huh?' he said dumbly. Wendy rolled her eyes. 'God dammit Jonny, you haven't heard a word I've said, have you?' She scolded Jonny like a naughty child who got too close to the hot stove.

'I'm sorry, OK!' he said, higher than usual, his voice breaking at the end. 'You can't just say, 'you killed someone' without expecting a reaction... from anyone decent anyway,' he said looking down again sadly.

She took a few seconds to answer, then said, 'Look... I know this has gotta be hard for you... excuse my 'straight to the point' work ethic... but it's just me. No offence intended, OK?' It wasn't really a question, more of a statement. She was trying though, Jonny thought.

'Yeah, I killed him... by accident,' Jonny said resignedly.

'Oh, I know it was by accident. We know most things, Jonny. You don't need to worry about that. Sometimes the only thing we need to know is why. But with this guy... clearly a complete dick hole, I might add, we knew already. It says it here, right in your file.' Wendy explained.

'Oh,' was all that Jonny said.

'Yeah. So...' Wendy began.

'Hang on... sorry Wendy,' Jonny interrupted. 'Is that the reason I'm here, right?' he continued.

'Yep,' she answered simply. 'Well... one of the reasons,' she continued.

Before Jonny could ask anything else, Wendy spoke again.

'Listen, hear me out, OK. So... yes, that is one of the

reasons you are here. Also, the woman...' she said, flicking through her notes.

'Which one?' he asked, bitterly.

She slapped her hand on one of the pages, almost in triumph. It was clear that Wendy had found the page she was looking for. She stated simply, 'Bettie.'

Jonny looked up at her in disbelief, his mouth open.

'What?' he breathed.

'Yeah,' replied Wendy, matter-of-factly. 'Your grandmother.'

'Why the hell am I hear because of my gran?' he questioned, anger rising within him like an uncoiling rattlesnake, ready to strike.

Wendy's eyes flickered down for a moment, then she looked up at him incredulously.

'Jonny, your gran has been an annoyance to you since your grandfather passed away, OK. Is that her fault though? As grandsons go, you were not the worse... I can assure you of that!' she said raising her eyebrows. 'However, you certainly weren't the best I'm afraid. You tended to be quite short with her, wouldn't engage, wouldn't make an effort and clearly preferred spending time with others,' Wendy continued, a little more delicately.

Before Jonny could reply, Wendy continued, 'Bettie needed attention. I get that she was a pain in the ass sometimes; old people can be like that, especially when they ask stupid questions, constantly. But she needed attention for a reason... you could have helped her and been more patient rather than lacklustre and irritable.

'You are a good guy... an understanding one... but you didn't expand that to your eldest family member.' She finished, trying to be as polite as possible, it seemed.

Jonny was quiet for some time... and then he looked up at

the bright light in the ceiling. A few tears began to run down his cheeks. He wiped them away quickly and looked down.

He sighed a long, slow sigh, like when someone realised where they had gone wrong.

'Shit. You're right. I feel terrible knowing that. She deserved better,' he said genuinely, a quiver of sadness in his voice.

'Don't worry,' she said. 'This is the bit of the job I hate the most. Decent people... such as yourself... never realise that the little things they missed or messed up in life are things that will come to haunt them in the next life,' she continued with a sad but reassuring smile. 'It hits home deep when they realise Jonny, just like how you're feeling now,' she added, picking up the cigarette packet.

'Right, you want another smoke?' she asked, clearly trying to lighten the mood with a completely different subject. Jonny appreciated the change in topic.

'Uh yeah, sure,' he replied, realising then that he hadn't noticed finishing the last one. There were two butts in the ashtray, so clearly, he had. 'I'm losing my fucking marbles,' he said with a grin as he took a cigarette from the proffered pack.

'Come work here, babe, you'll soon realise where you *really* loose it!' she said with a laugh.

Jonny smiled and chucked a little himself.

'So,' Jonny began, 'What about...' but before he could finish his sentence, Wendy interrupted with just one word. 'Hattie?' She blew a sharp cloud of blue smoke to her right, the smoke wafting around the room, creating a haze between them.

'Yeah,' he said quietly, looking down again. Jonny took a hard drag on his cigarette and did not look up.

He knew Hattie would come up. Except for Autumn, it was the guiltiest he had ever knowingly felt about something.

The douche bag he had killed by accident was an awful human being. He didn't deserve to die, Jonny was sure of that, but he didn't feel the same guilt as he did about Hattie.

Sure, he had felt guilty, especially in the months that led on from the incident but once he had moved and settled, he began to find peace, quite easily, he was ashamed to admit.

When Hattie had died though, it had broken him. Jonny had not taken this well at all.

He never told the police of him knowing her, all be it only for one night. He had never got over that either, which just fuelled his misery and anxiety.

Just days after he found out she was dead; he had begun to shut people out and become somewhat of a recluse. He began to drink more, smoke more and this wasn't just pertaining to cigarettes.

Weed made him less anxious certainly, but the flip side was he became paranoid. It was an unhealthy mixture.

One day, his sister had stopped in with her three children to see how he was.

When he opened the door, bleary eyed and dishevelled, he could see in her eyes that she regretted coming, as soon as he opened the door, and she took a look at him.

Jonny had never told anyone what had happened. He just bottled it up – looking back at it, he could see how dangerous that had been for his health, both physical and mental.

A mere four weeks after this tragedy, as it was a tragedy to Jonny, he met up with Doug, who had been an old university buddy. He was down in the South West, enjoying a few days away with his brother.

They had met at a local pub in a valley a few miles away from the Valley that Jonny called home.

It was a nice meal and made a change to get out. Doug

had been concerned about Jonny's appearance and general demeanour.

Jonny brushed it off and said he was having a hard time due to family troubles and an ex-girlfriend.

Doug seemed to accept that, mercifully, Jonny had thought. They then began to talk shop.

Doug confessed that he didn't just want to see Jonny to catch up on old times. He had a proposition for him and was keen to discuss it.

It turned out that Doug had set up a little photography agency in the Highlands of Scotland. The agency exclusively did shots of weather and wildlife for local papers and magazines. The focus was everything Scottish.

It made sense to Jonny as he knew Doug was half Scottish and had lived there in his teenage years with his father.

Doug didn't just want to show off his new venture though, he asked Jonny to join him in a joint partnership. He didn't need to put any money in, just work his magic in editorial and photo taking itself.

For that, Jonny would get forty-nine percent of the business and would be titled a director, the same as Doug.

Doug also confirmed that Jonny could come live with him in a luxurious two-bedroom apartment that he had leased at the same time as setting up the business. It was on the same premises, an old workshop converted beautifully for the business and the giant loft, being converted into a hip apartment.

Surprising even himself, Jonny jumped feet first into the idea once he had read over the proposal.

four weeks later he was packing his most important possessions in the truck and heading on his way to one of the most northern tips of Scotland.

He had rented the barn out on a six-month lease through a local estate agent. He had not rented out the workshop where he had found Hattie that time. He stored all his other belongings in there and had it secured professionally.

It had been fun living with someone again. Jonny had got himself together, even dated someone for a month or so.

He loved the work, and the business grew slowly. That being said, the overheads were massive, and Jonny found that after all the bills were paid, he didn't have much in the way of spending money. He was thankful he still had his old business on hiatus and the barn, which provided a healthy income.

Fast-forward around a year and Jonny was out searching for a new apartment because his old friend had fallen in love.

Now he was here. That is where it had ended, on a shitty, dark, Scottish night. He needed to know more... he needed to know what happened. But first, Hattie. As soon as he accepted that he was in Purgatory, he knew Hattie would be a major factor.

Jonny nervously took a drag on his cigarette and then stubbed it out in the tacky ashtray.

'OK, well I know why I am here with regards to Hattie,' he said quickly. 'You don't need to explain... I know I'm a piece of shit who kicked her out when she pleaded with me for help. I've kicked myself every day since, believe me,' he continued irritably.

'I know you have, Jonny,' Wendy said empathetically. 'You are here because of her also, you're right. But I need to add that you were in an extremely difficult situation there and a lot of people would have done the same,' Wendy continued, repeating 'a lot' firmly.

'Thank you,' Jonny said looking down and wiping a tear

away. He had so much built-up emotion over this, and it was like popping the cork on a fizzed-up bottle, telling someone, or at least discussing it with someone.

He sighed and smiled at Wendy who smiled back reassuringly.

'So...' he said straightening himself in his seat and taking a deep breath.

'What about Autumn,' he questioned.

'What about her?' Wendy replied, raising an eyebrow.

'What do you mean?' Jonny questioned, confused. 'Obviously she's the next reason I am here... the biggest I would have thought,' he considered aloud.

'Autumn has nothing to do with you being here Jonny, the files don't lie. What happened to her was not your fault,' Wendy said, her eyes focusing on Jonny intently.

CHAPTER 16

'Right... you've lost me,' Jonny said, as he stared at Wendy, an eyebrow raised, a look of complete bewilderment apparent on his face. 'How can that not be a reason... the main reason, that I am here?' he continued, frustration lacing his words like water lacing whiskey.

'Jonny, it's here in the damn file and it *wasn't* your fault!' Wendy replied hotly.

'Look,' she said more calmly. 'Autumn made her own decision to leave, yeah? You decided together to go for a walk and ended up screwing in that Wendy house, right?' she questioned, an eyebrow raised.

'Well yeah...' he said thoughtfully. 'It was a playhouse though,' he said with a small smile, flickering at the corners of his mouth. 'Smart ass,' she said with a lop-sided grin.

'Point is,' she continued, 'Autumn went into it of her own volition,' Wendy said simply. 'She also proceeded to get in that car and drive it; knowing full well, she was three sheets to the wind!' Wendy continued, extinguishing her cigarette in the ashtray.

'You know,' Wendy said, a smile playing at her lips, 'one good thing about the afterlife? This shit doesn't kill you anymore,' she continued with a laugh pointing at the cigarette packet.

Wendy had switched gears again and Jonny had to give her credit, the point he was trying to make, had been quashed fairly.

He shrugged his shoulders and smiled at Wendy, feeling the knots in his back and shoulders, that he had carried for so long, release significantly.

It was like a weight had been lifted off his shoulders, Atlas could appreciate that quip, Jonny thought, his smile turning into a grin.

'What?' questioned Wendy curiously, her smile now also turning to a grin, mirroring Jonny's.

'Nothing,' Jonny said with a laugh. 'It's just... the flood of relief in my veins... I feel like I just...' He stopped, trying to think of the right words.

'You feel like you just took a massive dump,' Wendy said, straight faced, then burst out laughing.

'Yeah!' Jonny said joining her laughter, 'that's pretty much it!'

'Good,' Wendy said smiling. 'Now,' she said, all business again.

'Let's get back to it,' she continued. 'I am not gonna go through the rest as it's just riffraff bullshit that just adds up to the reason, you're here...nothing interesting, OK?' she said, her question more of a statement.

Jonny nodded, still sailing on his high from learning he wasn't responsible for Autumn's death.

Wendy closed the file and began to type, methodically on the vintage computer's keyboard.

'Is that a vintage Mac from the 1980s?' Jonny questioned.

Wendy looked away from the screen with a smirk. 'Yep. Hey, if it ain't broke don't fix it! That's the motto round here, son, so get used to it,' she said with a laugh.

Jonny could swear that if Wendy had a tattoo on her forehead, it would say psych and have a middle finger next to it for good measure. He grinned to himself at the thought.

She continued to type for a while and then looked at him again.

'Right. Just some bureaucratic bullshit to get out of the

way now Jonny,' she said sighing.

'Can you confirm your name and date of birth, last known address and give me a password that you will always remember?' she continued tiredly.

Jonny obliged, and then Wendy began to use the equally archaic looking mouse, to slide down the pages she was reading.

'No wheel on that mouse,' Jonny said with a grin.

'Ha! I wish!' she said with a snort.

'Right. Here we go Jonny. Last bit from the paperwork side that I need to do with you now, OK?' she said, again as a statement, not a question.

Wendy hesitated before speaking again and Jonny's high began to ebb, replaced with concern.

'What?' he questioned when Wendy didn't continue.

'The next bit... it's umm... I have to formally explain to you how you died, Jonny. I then need you to confirm you accept it... I have to click a button with a tick box in it.' She said this delicately and remarkably quietly for Wendy, who was clearly a no nonsense, loud individual.

'OK,' Jonny said nervously, knowing that would inevitably come up.

Wendy brightened then, the serious tone all but gone, a laugh replaced it. 'Hey, don't worry, you weren't murdered or found with your pants down or taking a dump... it was all standard, above board!' she said with a grin.

Her features then went serious, and she brushed a hand through her hair, her fringe standing up for a few seconds, making her bob cut look almost amusing.

'That day you were house hunting... or apartment hunting, should I say,' she began.

'The last one before you were gonna head for the one outta

town, remember?' she said, this time an actual question.

'Yeah,' Jonny confirmed simply. Funnily enough, he remembered that the last apartment, his least favourite, had made him feel funny when he had exited the communal hallway on the ground floor.

The building had been nice on the outside, but tired inside. It was an old Victorian terrace that was like five stories in total. It was the large loft apartment that he had gone to view.

The layout had been awful, and it was worn out. This was the reason Jonny had left fairly quickly. He had wanted to get a head start on the journey to the last property as it was quite a distance from this one, considering rush hour was in full flow outside.

'I'll try and be delicate, Jonny, but as you've gathered by now, it's not my forte,' Wendy said with a kind smile. 'We always try to be careful around the subject of death itself, as it can be quite distressing knowing what your last moments were like, especially considering you won't remember the final one,' she continued quietly.

'It's OK, Wendy, go for it, I'm a big boy,' Jonny said, a false smile plastered on his face. In truth, he was nervous about finding out the details of his untimely demise.

'Sure,' she said with a smile and then sighed and sat up straighter.

'You slipped halfway down, whilst you headed for the ground floor Jonny,' she said delicately, her hazel eyes showing a hint of concern, her mouth going involuntarily into a grimace.

'Right,' Jonny said, drawing the word out slowly as if he needed the time to process it's meaning.

'The steps were wet from a leak that pooled on the third-floor landing. It seems it was just below a window, hence the leak,' she said thoughtfully.

She scanned the computer screen, moving the pages down again with the old mouse, the plastic casing yellowed with age, Jonny noticed.

'Yeah,' she said in finality. 'So... you slipped there and tumbled down the staircase to the second floor where you literally broke your neck against the solid brick wall opposite. You had also sustained internal bleeding during the fall and cracked your head open, losing a lot of blood,' she said, pushing back from the desk slightly and taking a deep breath.

Jonny looked at her quizzically. He thought for a moment and then said, 'what about the journey here? I mean I remember leaving, albeit a bit hazy, I admit,' he said, placing a hand subconsciously on his chin, running his fingers through his beard.

'That was all after you passed Jonny. You died right away,' Wendy replied, delicately.

'So, the drive here and everything was...' he started but couldn't find the words.

'Yep,' she said matter-of-factly. 'It was all your journey here, hun!' she continued with a smile. 'Crazy I know!' Wendy said with a roll of her eyes, putting a hand up in the air, briefly. The gesture symbolised 'who knows' it seemed.

Jonny smiled and mimicked her, by raising his arm in the air briefly too.

'Screw it. Done now hey,' Jonny said finally with a tired smile, understanding and acceptance clear in his voice.

'The thing is, Jonny...and this moves me on to my next part of this meeting, about how things are here... we don't really know how this shit works! I mean, who the fuck are we, mere mortals... or were mere mortals, to question the universe, to question the cosmos!' she said with a matter-of-fact look on her face. 'We are just flies buzzing around shit, my friend,' she continued, raising both hands this time and then suddenly she slapped them down on the desk.

'Anyway, let's get on,' she said in finality.

'For this bit though... you're gonna need a smoke and a strong drink... as this shit will really make your dingle tingle,' she said with a grin.

CHAPTER 17

A stiff glass of bourbon was placed in front of Jonny. He liked all things American, so this suited him perfectly.

Wendy placed a fresh pack of cigarettes down next to the glass. 'Your very own pack,' she said with a sarcastic grin, wiggling her eyebrows.

Jonny lit one with the lighter that Wendy had also provided. A comical looking naked girl lighter. Jonny smirked as he paid closer attention to it.

He pressed down on the obnoxiously large breasts and laughed when the nipples lit up red. The flame burst out the naked woman's mouth, which opened massively wide with the click of the button - this, Jonny thought was a little darker than the rest of the comical lighter.

He lit his cigarette and took a long drag. With the same hand he grabbed the glass and took a long swig of the amber liquid. It looked like tree sap almost.

He regretted doing this instantly though, for two reasons.

Firstly, the large mouthful of bourbon burnt his throat; it felt like someone had scratched his oesophagus with a nail file.

Secondly, because he was holding the cigarette between his fingers of the same hand, the smoke got far too close to his eyes; (something that Jonny did regularly and never learnt from) it burnt them with the cigarettes thick, chemical smoke.

His eyes began to stream tears. It felt like someone had sprayed pepper spray in them for a few seconds.

Once this had passed, he took another timid sip of the drink, making sure he took his time. He also ensured that the cigarette was leant against one of the ashtrays sides before doing so.

'So,' he said to Wendy, wiping one eye, from the last remnants of the poisonous smoke. 'This next bit is gonna make me shit the bed, metaphorically speaking?' he quizzed with a grin.

'Pretty much,' Wendy said with a smirk.

'OK then,' Jonny replied simply. 'Hit me with it, boss!' he continued.

Wendy looked at him for a few seconds, shuffled the paperwork in front of her around and lit her own cigarette, from her packet.

Jonny had the distinct feeling that she was procrastinating.

She took an enormous drag on the cigarette and blew it out slowly. Wendy leant her head back so that the smoke curled upwards.

Jonny saw the blue silky smoke exit her nose in two thin streams that almost looked like two waterfalls, lazily falling to a serene lake – the difference being they curled upwards, of course.

Wendy slowly brought her head forward, so that she could again make eye contact with Jonny.

She frowned slightly, almost imperceptibly and began. 'This is Purgatory. Known by many names... none of them right or wrong, including Purgatory itself. It's just what we tend to call it here... in this sector anyway.'

Wendy leant back in her chair; it reclined somewhat and creaked slightly.

She didn't have a bourbon, but Jonny noticed a mug next to the archaic computer screen. It read 'Best Mom'. Jonny assumed it had some sort of hot beverage in it... that being said it was probably freezing cold by now, he mused.

She looked up at the ceiling and continued to talk. 'There are many sectors here. Endless sectors really like there are endless offices. The sectors work together and have people like Bob, who keeps the machine firing on all cylinders. We call them runners, why you may ask? Because they spend all their time running around from pillar to post, giving us updates and bringing information that we need, such as files.' She indicated to Jonny's file, that was still sat (now closed) on her desk.

'The runners know everything that is going on in the sector. They are connected to other runners so that we have an overall picture of what the hell is going on in this crazy place,' she continued, ending with a sigh.

Wendy continued to stare upwards and didn't say anything else. Jonny assumed this was his turn to speak, even just for affirmation that he so far understood... as well as he could that is.

'Right, with you so far, chief,' he said light heartedly. He had to muster this however as it was indeed quite a lot to take in.

'Now, Jonny, like me you're probably not the sharpest tool in the box but you are switched on enough and you're street smart, I'm sure,' she stated matter-of-factly.

'Geez, don't sugar coat it, Wend,' he said with a small laugh.

She smiled at him tiredly and continued, 'I said that as the next bit is a bit of a mind fuck... but you have to remember... we are not on earth anymore... effectively anyway. This is another plane of existence... it's another life altogether, in fact.'

Wendy seemed quite animated now. Jonny couldn't tell if she was excited or worried.

Before he could ponder this any further, she continued. 'This shit hole diner is not Purgatory, Jonny.' She put her finger to the light dimple in her chin then and said, 'Let me rephrase that. Purgatory is not *just* this diner. I mean you'd have to be thick as dogshit to think that the cesspit behind you,' she paused to point at the closed door that led back into the diner. 'With all of thirty odd people in it, was the entirety of Purgatory. Look at this endless line of offices in all directions... would it all be for one shit hole diner?' she questioned, finishing with a laugh.

Jonny laughed too, realising the absurdity of it. He had already assumed something along these lines, but it was good to have clarification.

'There are countless places just like the one behind you. Countless. They are not all diners either. There are many different types... I don't even know how many... probably thousands and thousands, if not millions,' She said, again subconsciously fingering her chin, as she considered this comment.

'I only work here, at this diner; but after speaking to Bob and some others, I know that there are places extremely similar to ours... and then on the other end of the scale you'll find places like in the movies,' She continued thoughtfully.

'You know what I mean, Jonny... dark, dank places... in the woods... perpetual darkness or dusk at least... hooded figures moping around... mist everywhere; that sort of thing,' She said, the last words quick and light-hearted. Jonny had to laugh at this.

'If there's loads of choice, why the hell am I here and not somewhere like that nightmare you just described?' he questioned, shaking his head, albeit with a smile.

'Did I say there's a choice?' she replied simply. Before Jonny could utter a word, Wendy spoke again. 'There is a system... an algorithm or some shit, that decides these things. Now don't ask me how it works or any bullshit like that as I *don't* know. What I can tell you is this crazy system is well above our pay grades... it's not for us to understand, OK? All you need to know is it works, and it is *never* wrong. Whatever the cosmos does to decide these factors is a mystery, like I said. But all I can say is it's like the decision to put you in Purgatory rather than anywhere else...' she paused briefly and pointed up and then down.

'It factors in everything and spits out, 'Subject A goes to location B'. So that's why you're here!' she finished by breathing a big sigh (of what seemed relief, Jonny thought).

'Some luck that I came here where Autumn is,' Jonny said thoughtfully, more to himself than anyone else.

'That is very true', Wendy replied.

'You pointed up and down... does that mean...' Jonny began but trailed off.

'You got it, champ,' Wendy said crossing her arms. Before Jonny could say anything else, Wendy spoke again.

'We don't call it Heaven and Hell here, OK? Why may you ask? Well, like Purgatory, there are countless names for both... it can depend just on the region or culture you come from... safe to say it's up and down,' She said flatly, no nonsense in her voice.

'Paradise, mecca... whatever you want to call it... it's all the same... everyone has a little bit right about all these places. It's safe to say though, that one is good, one is bad, and one is... here,' Wendy paused and looked around with both her hands up in the air, as if to show Jonny where they were.

'This is the middle... the waiting place... the... hmm,' she paused again and looked thoughtful, then continued more slowly; 'This place that we... in this sector, call purgatory... is a gateway.'

CHAPTER 18

'A gateway?' Jonny asked, thoughtfully, more to himself than Wendy. 'That's a fairly apt word for it, Wend,' he continued.

'Yeah, we think so,' she replied with a tired smile.

After a moment, another thought crossed Jonny's mind, and he decided to ask Wendy before any more information filled and overwhelmed his tired brain.

'So... down...' he questioned, as he pointed down, his eyebrows raised as if he was silently pressing Wendy to explain more.

'Yeah,' she said firmly. 'Not a place you want to end up from what I hear,' she continued seriously, without an ounce of humour in her tone.

Jonny felt he wasn't going to get more information than that. It may have been because Wendy genuinely didn't know any more than what she had already said, or that he wasn't privy to more information.

After all, he thought, he hadn't been sent there and therefore, technically didn't need to know anything about it. All he needed to know is it was bad, and Wendy had made that quite clear.

Jonny switched gears. 'The entrance to the diner,' he began, seriously, eyeing Wendy with interest.

'Was all that stuff earlier really true? Was it really the door to Hell... sorry... down? If I had walked out for a smoke... would that have been it for me?' he questioned, a frown deep on his brow. A bead of sweat ran down his forehead and he wiped it away, quickly. Subconsciously (Jonny thought), if true, he was a little more freaked out about being so close to 'hell' then he let on.

Wendy did not answer right away. She twisted her chair this way and that, so that she was facing the office to her left. A moment later, she faced the office to the right.

She's procrastinating again, Jonny thought.

With a sigh, she finally stopped fidgeting and focused on Jonny.

'Yes,' she said quietly, 'it is true, I'm afraid,' Wendy continued, sombrely.

'The last thing you want to do is walk through that door, OK?' she said a little louder and far firmer.

'I have seen people do just that... before I could stop them or talk them out of it... its heart-breaking, Jonny,' she continued, this time quieter again, but with so much emotion in her voice, Jonny thought she may begin to cry.

It seemed Wendy was concerned about this too. She wiped her eyes quickly, sat up straight and gave herself a little shake, barely perceivable to Jonny.

'Right! Let's move on, hun, I haven't got all of eternity to sit here with you,' she said, brightening. As if an afterthought, she became somewhat serious again and added, 'That's the score with the front door. Do not go near it. Simple. Capeesh?' Almost instantly, she changed the subject. Jonny had no chance to answer, even if he was meant to. He looked at Wendy, slightly bewildered.

'Time wise, we don't give numbers here. If you spend your time wisely, it will go significantly quicker than you would think possible. Likewise... if you mope around and make the worst of your time... it will pretty much take as long as the actual time you have here,' she stated matter-of-factly.

'Oh, and before you ask, yes, this new plane of existence runs differently on time. You can genuinely manipulate it, by spending your time here wisely,' she continued.

Before Jonny could utter a single syllable, she began again.

'I mean, how the hell did some poor bastards do a thousand years or so here? Simple. Using their time wisely and making the best of it. You do that and you can make that thousand years feel like a tiny fraction of the actual time. To be honest, Jonny, time is a human construct and it's not actually real... we just made it up to help us... like any tool or machine.' Wendy had begun to speak with more enthusiasm, Jonny noticed.

'That is why it is so easy to play with time here; to your advantage,' she finished.

'So... I won't know how long I am here... it's not a thousand years right?' Jonny asked after a moment, worry clear in his voice.

Wendy laughed. 'Babe, you're on the diet cola side of your term here... don't worry about it... you can do it standing on your head, I promise!' she said smiling, reassuringly.

'We put people into categories, much like the cosmos or whatever the hell it is, does when deciding which Purgatory, a person will go to when they are here. Example being, yours was here, an American style diner,' she said this with conviction and Jonny felt he was meant to have understood more from the comment then he really did.

Wendy could clearly sense the confusion and the brewing questions. She sighed and continued, 'The categories are confidential, OK? Just know this, we put you into them like time slots of the time you need to be here. It's like a point score for what you did to end up here. That's how it is calculated.'

Jonny was about to ask the obvious question (he thought at least), before Wendy spoke again, clearly guessing that would be next.

'You're in a lower category OK, Jonny. The green section, the lowest bar one which is white. You'd never make it to white, however. Reason being... white is reserved for those who have extraordinary circumstances. There are several categories in each coloured section, but you are, thankfully in the green,' she said with a smile.

'That's all I get to know?' He asked incredulously.

'Yep,' Wendy said simply, not noticing or perhaps not caring about the tone in which Jonny spoke.

'Look, that's all I *can* tell you and to be honest, even if I could tell you more, I've told you as much as you need to know, really,' she said with finality, and with no sign of humour in her voice.

Jonny decided he was not going to learn anymore about this and that he should just settle in for the long haul, do his time and move on to whatever was next. Suddenly, concern crossed both his mind and his features. His brow creased deeply.

'Wendy. Can I just check... after all this...' he began, his arms waving around the room as if to illustrate this was the place in question.

'After all this...' he repeated. 'We do... go... up, right?' he asked slowly, almost stretching the question out. It was as if he was afraid to find out the answer, he thought.

Wendy smiled at him then, warmly.

'Don't worry, hun. When you've done your time here... just like the books and the movies say... it's your turn to go up and head into Paradise, that I can guarantee,' Wendy said. She said this with such conviction that Jonny felt his body completely relax – it was as if he had just turned to blancmange... all his bones melting, and he was this completely relaxed puddle of warm goo!

'That's awesome to hear, Wendy,' he said simply, a relaxed sigh, slowly leaving his lips, like a whisper.

A thought occurred to Jonny, and he eyed Wendy with interest. She noticed and frowned slightly, then smiled.

'What now?' she questioned, light heartedly.

'Well...' Jonny began, scratching his beard, thoughtfully.

'What's your score, Wend? I mean... how did you get this gig?' he continued; interest clear upon his features.

'That my friend is an interesting and weird story... I'd be happy to tell you some time, but the big question is... do you really want to hear it?' she asked, the last bit with a smirk, almost a challenge, Jonny thought.

'Tell me now! I'd love to hear your story. I mean you know all about me and if we are gonna be stuck here together for a long time, I'd love to know how you got here...' Jonny said enthusiastically. He quickly added, 'If you don't mind that is.' A sheepish grin appearing on his rugged, but handsome face.

'OK, OK!' Wendy said raising both her hands in surrender. She rolled her eyes and continued. 'To be honest, it's a good subject as it amalgamates with the next bit, I was gonna explain to you anyway.'

Jonny raised an eyebrow, questionably at this, but said nothing as he didn't want to stop the hypothetical train, now that it was rolling.

'Working here, right? All of us are Purgatory residence, from one time or another. A bit like prison, most of us who use our time wisely and are generally a benefit to the society they find themselves part of, get a chance to leave early,' she said this fairly quickly, and Jonny realised that this must have happened to her at some point.

She took a deep breath, as if she was about to dive into the ocean and continued. 'The deal is always the same, for those that get offered a chance to leave early... for good behaviour, let's call it.' She laughed a little at this. A reference to the way it works in prisons on earth, Jonny thought, seeing the irony.

'You get offered three choices,' she continued, matter-of-factly. 'You'll get these choices too Jonny, if you keep your nose clean and use your time as best you can,' she added.

'The first choice... stay here and do your time, then off to Paradise. Simple,' she stated.

'The second choice... is to go back to living. That is to be reborn... reincarnated, effectively,' she said with an odd smile. 'There is a caveat though my friend!' she said suddenly raising a finger, high in the air.

'You won't remember anything, *and* you don't know where you're gonna end up. You could be born a billionaire's son, who ends up curing cancer! On the other hand, you could end up as some poor bastard, living in a third world country who ends up making kidnapping and murder his or her career,' she finished, thoughtfully.

'Not only that but when you are... appraised, let's call it, when you die...' she said, appraised with air quotes, Jonny noticed, amused.

'Your old life gets tallied up with your new life... this means it's much more difficult to make it to the promised land straight off... there is much more chance you'll end up right back here, with an even longer term... or worse that is,' she finished, the last comment quiet, her eyes averting Jonny's.

'Pretty shitty deal to be honest, Wend,' was all Jonny could think to say.

'Yeah, your right, hun!' she answered, a little more lightly.

There was a pause then and they both seemed to be deep in thought.

Jonny then spoke up and prompted her to continue. 'The third option, Wend?'

She sighed and smiled at him, then said tiredly, 'The third option... is to work here...'

Jonny was taken aback by this. It should have been obvious, but he was shocked all the same.

'You work here, for an undetermined amount of time... it is... the same amount of time you have left here in Purgatory.' Wendy said, pausing in thought.

Before she could continue, Jonny butted in and exclaimed, 'Really! Why would you do that?'

'Let me finish, buddy, geez!' she said, exasperated.

'Like I said, you have to serve your time here... working... *but* you also get to leave for Paradise.' She finished with a lopsided grin. Jonny guessed she was looking at him like that, as she knew his face would be a picture.

She laughed and continued before Jonny could ask any questions, 'It's like shift work, Jonny. You come here for a bit, then you're let go for a bit, back up to Paradise, home. Once you've done your time, you don't come back here... simple... you're done, enjoy, bye, sayonara.'

Now Jonny could see... it made sense, and he quickly concluded that this was indeed what Wendy had done. Just for confirmation, he asked, 'So... you did this, right?'

'No flies on you, hun!' she said with a laugh.

Jonny laughed too. 'Only way I was gonna see my kids again... no damn way would I have chosen anything else!' she added.

Jonny frowned at this and then timidly asked, 'Wendy... what happened to you... I mean how did you die... and how did you end up here?'

'Well... it's a long story Jonny... let me refill your glass and

I'll tell you, screw it... think we've got time right?' she said, sarcastically, grinning.

As she stood and went over to the filing cabinet she continued to talk, but over her shoulder.

'I killed my ex-husband.' It was like a gunshot going off in the office.

Jonny looked at her, his mouth open. He said nothing, just stared at her back as she opened the filing cabinet and retrieved the bottle of bourbon. She then began to refill the glass on top of the cabinet. She stopped for a moment, clearly in thought. She then moved back towards the desk. She picked up the mug on the table and smiled at it warmly. She then downed whatever was in it... clearly not the nicest, as her face was a mask of clear disgust.

She then filled the mug with bourbon too. As she put the bottle back, she continued to talk. 'He was truly the worst, Jonny. A controlling, vicious and violent asshole. I'd had enough for years. Then in seventy-eight I met this girl... I'd always been kind of interested in both if you get my meaning... we fell in love, and she gave me the mental strength to leave that bastard. I did, just six weeks after meeting her. Took my three girls and just left... all we had was a small suitcase each... but we didn't care, we were free.' Wendy seemed to go off into her memories for a split second. After a long pause, she continued.

'Anyway, he was livid as you can imagine. Came after us. Sadly... he found us.' She said as she sat heavily in the chair, sighing.

'Is... is that how you died, Wendy? From injuries sustained by him when he found you?' Jonny asked delicately.

Wendy looked up then. She had been staring at her mug, a sad smile playing at her lips.

She gave a short, harsh laugh and said, 'No, no! he stabbed me... both me and Kathy... that was my... my lover,' she said this last word, almost shyly.

'In self-defence, I stabbed him back...luckily cutting his femoral artery... the prick,' she continued. 'He bled out and died. Simple. That's why I am here... well the main reason in any case.'

'Right... that's terrible, Wendy, awful... but... how did you... you know, pass?' Jonny asked quietly.

Wendy waited a long time to answer, just looking at her mug. Then she said, in not much more than a murmur, 'you sure you want to hear this, Jonny?'

'Yes,' he said clearly.

'OK then,' Wendy replied with raised eyebrows. Her tone made Jonny think she was almost saying, 'your funeral, pal!'

Wendy sat up a little straighter then. She took a large swig of the amber liquid, grimacing somewhat. She then lit a cigarette from the packet in front of her. She took a long drag, blew it out sharply and eyed Jonny. They both sat there like that for a little while... Jonny thought he could feel the tension growing in the room. It became almost palpable. He felt he could reach out and touch it like a damp mist.

Wendy then spoke up, her tone serious and somewhat daunting to Jonny. 'I was murdered Jonny. Me and my three daughters, brutally murdered. You wanted to know... so this is what happened...'

CHAPTER 19
WENDY'S STORY

She put the Chrysler into reverse and backed out of the hospital parking lot, slowly.

As Wendy moved the column shifter of the station wagon into gear, she turned and smiled at the passenger beside her on the bench seat.

Kathy returned the smile, clearly tired, and a little worse for wear, but happy; Wendy was fairly sure of that.

Six months it had taken to get to this point. Six horrific months to get Kathy well enough to come home. Six months for Wendy to get her head around what had happened.

The trial had just begun and according to her court appointed lawyer, it was an open and shut case. They expected it to take mere weeks, and then it would all be behind them. No one, even the prosecution (she had heard), thought that this would be anything more than a 'moving through the motions' kind of case.

It was self-defence, with witnesses in Wendy's home. The home she happily shared with her children and Kathy. The home they were now about to return to.

Wendy felt giddy with anticipation of it all being over. She could not wait! She had no qualms about the trial and knew it was just a process that needed to be completed. Her asshole ex-husband had tried to kill them both, and she had reacted in the only way possible at the time. That was it. Simple. The lawyers said that it was the simplest type of case, regarding homicide.

Kathy and Wendy had not been together long, but Wendy

just knew, that this was the one, that this was right. It was a whirlwind romance, and it was one that she was confident would stand the test of time, like a beautiful old building, growing more elegant with age.

Wendy sighed a big happy sigh and looked out of the windshield at the blazing Utah sun. It was a glorious day and one that she felt was the first day (officially) of her new life. Nothing could ruin this feeling... this day... she thought.

She turned to look at Kathy. Kathy was a short but solid unit of a woman. She was fun loving, had a funky grey and black hair cut that almost resembled an Elvis style.

She was very retro too; she loved to dress in men's fifties clothes.

God, she loved that woman. Wendy beamed a smile as she stole another glance at Kathy.

Wendy kept an eye on the road and lent over slightly to place a hand on Kathy's thigh.

Oddly, Kathy wriggled and seemed to be uncomfortable with the touch, that was meant to be loving and show the commitment of Wendy's feelings for her.

Wendy slowed the station wagon somewhat and looked at Kathy properly. It was the first time since getting in the car that she had really focused on her. Wendy quickly realised that Kathy did not look well. She looked slightly grey, perhaps tired and... anxious... maybe unhappy.

She kept picking at a thread on her black pants. Wendy noticed her nails were bitten down to the fingertips.

Concern was abundant on Wendy's face then. She pulled the car off the road suddenly, into the back parking lot of some hardware store.

She shoved the Chrysler into park and moved her whole body so that she sat side on, facing Kathy.

The Chryslers big block V8 purred away, almost silently, like a monster, sat in the dark, waiting to jump on its prey. Wendy had left it running so that they didn't melt like popsicles in the sun, thanks to the powerful AC being up fairly high.

Kathy continued to stare out the window, an almost thousand-yard stare coming from her grey blue unfocused eyes.

'Earth to Kathy!' Wendy said jovially. She instantly regretted it however as Kathy jumped slightly, turned to face Wendy, with a look of pure anxiety upon her features.

Wendy's face fell into a frown, deep lines appearing on her forehead, in concern.

'What is wrong Kathy? I thought you would be so happy to be out of that place. You look like you're waiting for the mob to take out a hit on you!' she said, making the last part sound much lighter than she felt. The truth was, Wendy had not seen Kathy like this before, and she was worried.

'I'm... I'm sorry baby,' was all that Kathy said, in a quiet, croaky voice. Wendy continued to stare at her as Kathy looked from the front windshield to the rear and back to Wendy. She continued to do this periodically.

'What is wrong, Kathy?' Wendy asked again, firmer this time and far more seriously.

Kathy took a long breath and then said, 'I'm ill, Wend. All was going great at the hospital... the quacks kept getting me to do these weird tests. They clearly didn't want me to worry... but I could tell they were concerned.'

She paused then watching Wendy with a side glance. She seemed almost afraid to continue. Before Wendy could speak however, Kathy did.

'It's final. It's diagnosed after all the tests. I found out yesterday. I'm sorry,' she said quite robotically but the last words... 'I'm Sorry' were not just genuine, the words were almost pleading for Wendy to believe Kathy.

'Look, whatever it is, babe, we can work it out. Don't worry! Just tell me what the doctors said to you. Tell me what they diagnosed, OK?' Wendy said gently, placing a hand on Kathy's left shoulder.

Kathy started slightly and focused on Wendy. This made Wendy really worried. Kathy was not the jumpy type at all. She was the opposite. She had more balls than every guy Wendy had ever met. She was always the life of the party and always playing pranks and having a generally fun time. This was not her Kathy, no way, Wendy thought.

'I'm dangerous, Wendy,' was all that Kathy said. She said it with finality and with a seriousness that Wendy had never heard from Kathy. Also, Kathy never 'full named' her – it was a joke between them; Kathy knew that she hated being called Wendy. It had to be babe, or hun or sweet or Wend... whatever... just not Wendy. Not by Kathy.

'What?' was all that Wendy could say. She couldn't hide the incredulous look that was on her face.

'I'm nuts! OK!' Kathy blurted, a tear running down her cheek. 'It's official, Wend, I'm a fucking Paranoid Schizophrenic... and I am dangerous.' The tears ran freely now after this statement. Kathy looked like a broken woman.

'I have to take these new anti-psychotic meds and get what they call 'community-based care,' I dunno what I'm gonna do!' Kathy almost cried out the last words. Wendy looked deeply worried. She slid over the bench and hugged Kathy tightly, shushing her cries. She hung on hoping to comfort this rock of a woman, Wendy's rock. She cried too then. She couldn't help it. Kathy was broken; she could tell.

Wendy knew this was a bad sign.

Regardless, she straightened, wiped away her tears and said brightly, 'Don't worry, baby. We will get through this. I'll help with the meds and look... if you don't have to be in a ward or anything... they must think you're not doing too badly, right?'

A hint of a grin played on Kathy's dry and cracked lips for a split second but then it was gone.

'Hun, it's not safe. Trust me. I've looked into this and asked a bunch of questions since yesterday. With women it tends to get worse as they age. I'm in the relatively early stages... its gonna get bad... you don't wanna be stuck with me, you need to forget me and move on!' Kathy said, her heart clearly breaking, Wendy thought.

Wendy swallowed the lump in her throat, that threatened to start her crying all over again.

'I love you and I don't care about this thing... whatever it is... we've been through a lifetime of hell already in just a few months! We will beat it, OK?' Wendy said firmly.

'That's why I love you, baby.' Kathy said. A full grin actually showing this time, her white teeth almost sparkling, Wendy thought.

That was her Kathy, Wendy thought, satisfied and content. She smiled, and then she leant over and kissed Kathy. It was a long loving kiss. She felt the hairs on the back of her neck rise at this sudden, intense and passionate moment. From her reaction, Kathy seemed to feel it also.

'Let's get you home,' Wendy whispered into Kathy's ear, leaning back to show her vivacious grin.

'Lets,' replied Kathy simply, running a hand through her slick backed hair.

She turned then, just as Wendy put the car back into drive

and began to pull out. 'Thank you, Wend. You're an angel,' she said quietly. It was clear she meant it deeply and all Wendy could do was smile and pat Kathy's thigh.

A short way down the road, Kathy made a sort of snort noise, that perhaps had been a laugh.

Wendy glanced at her sideways, smiling. Her smile faded quickly however when she realised that Kathy was staring into the mirror of the sun vizor. She was almost imperceptibly nodding, and her eyes were raised as if agreeing with something someone had just stated.

Wendy turned round briefly to look behind her; a crazy notion as she knew it was just the two of them in the car. She did it all the same though.

The look in Kathy's eyes made Wendy wish that there was indeed someone else in the car.

CHAPTER 20
WENDY'S STORY CONTINUED

It was dark. It was cold. It stunk to high heaven. She tried to move her hands. Not an option. The same with her legs. She pushed her head back and forth.

There was some give behind her, as if it was somewhat softer than in front of her; that was solid, maybe wood?

Wendy began to panic. It came on so clear and strong, that she literally shook. Afraid that she may end up catatonic, she forced herself to breathe slowly. Long, deep breaths. In and out.

She continued to do this and after a minute she had slowed her breathing and had begun to relax a little – it was difficult though as it dawned on her quickly that her mouth was taped shut.

She had learnt breathing techniques during a weekend retreat she had attended a few years ago. She had gone with a friend; they both attended to try and learn coping techniques for dealing with their deadbeat husbands.

What a waste of time, it's not like it helped stop a fist, hey? Ironically though, it was sure helping now, Wendy thought, bitterly.

Now that Wendy was a little more relaxed, she began to focus her mind and try to remember what had happened.

It was a Tuesday... early evening... that, she knew. She had come home from her cleaning job early. One of her girls, had called and had sounded worried. Kathy was significantly worse that week and it seemed this evening was the worse yet.

It had only been a few months since they had left the hospital, where Wendy had promised to look after Kathy.

She knew in her heart, that Kathy was getting worse and quickly. She knew that she should really take Kathy in and get her institutionalised. Wendy couldn't bring herself to do it though. She had made a promise... a vow.

Also, Kathy was often, absolutely fine. Her normal, fun-loving self.

This put Wendy's mind significantly off kilter – when she was close to taking her in, she would change her mind completely as Kathy was suddenly fine.

It was such hard work on her and the girls.

She felt so guilty as the girls were suffering, she was sure. They wouldn't say anything, but she could tell... a mother knows.

Jessie was seven and strong willed like her mother. She loved Kathy and was similar to Wendy, in the fact that she just wanted to care for her and bury her head in the sand, assuming it would all be OK.

Sara and Tilly were not so accepting of Kathy's condition. Twin girls... ten going on thirty – they thought Kathy was an issue and that their mum should get her help. Even when she seemed fine, the twins were increasingly cautious around Kathy. They would stay in their room and make as little contact with the rest of the family as possible.

Wendy's mind was beginning to clear of the fog now. She remembered coming back early after Jessie had phoned her.

Her mind clouded again then and she head butted the solid material in front of her in frustration. It was mere inches from her face. She noticed then that the smell of wood and earth, assaulted her senses. The feeling of the solid item in front of her, although seemingly wood, seemed to have a vail over it. It was almost like it had a decorative cloth attached to it.

Before her mind could wonder and turn back into panic, she focused again, squeezing her eyes shut, tightly.

She had parked... rushed to the front door and flung it open.

She remembered now... it had been a shock. The house had been... like a bomb site. You would have been forgiven for thinking they had been burgled.

She had shouted out for her daughters... for Kathy. No response.

She remembered panicking... she rushed through the ground floor of the house checking everywhere. The master bedroom had been empty...there was no sign of anyone.

Wendy then headed for the stairs. She remembered rushing up the first few steps and almost stumbling. Then, she slowed, nearly to a stop.

She couldn't say why, but she remembered this immeasurable feeling of absolute dread... almost a sixth sense.

She continued up the stairs slowly. It was as if she was climbing to meet her demise, climbing to the top of a bridge that she would surely be pushed off of. The crashing waves below meeting her at an unfathomable speed, in her last few moments on this earth.

The lights were switched off on the upstairs landing. She also noticed how hot it was in the house... the AC was off. She flicked the light switch, and nothing happened. The power was out... or cut... by someone.

Tears began to well up in Wendy's eyes and she struggled to see as she stumbled down the hallway towards the children's bedrooms.

She got to Jessie's first. She pushed the door open slowly. The brightly painted pink room was bathed in natural light from the large window.

Mercifully, the room was empty. Wendy briefly checked under the bed and in the closet, but it was as she thought, empty.

She left the bedroom and headed further down the hallway, past the den, past the bathroom and to the final door, the twins room.

She again slowly pushed the door open. This time it was fairly dark, the curtains were still pulled closed.

There were two lumps in the two single beds in front of her. For a fleeting moment, Wendy just thought the girls were sleeping, perhaps taking a nap.

She walked in and as she got closer though, she realised, something was wrong. She slowed her approach and whispered the girl's names. There was no answer.

When she was next to Tilly's bed, she smelt a faint coppery odour. Urgency in her movements, she carefully pulled back the duvet.

Wendy's breath, caught in her throat. She let out a croaky scream, that seemed to be not much more than a whisper.

Everything seemed to turn into slow motion. Tears rolled down her cheeks. She felt utter anguish and hopelessness as she stared down at the broken body of her daughter.

Tilly had multiple stab wounds to her torso. Caked blood was all over the bed sheets and duvet. It was not yet congealed but Tilly's skin was cold to the touch.

She whipped her hand back in shock at this and then realising there was also blood on her fingers. She cried out.

Wendy found her voice then and screamed, 'Help!' The sound was so loud and strained, it felt as if her vocal cords were stretched.

In her devastated, panicked state, she almost dived over to the other bed and found Sara in the same, unbearable condition.

She felt her heart physically ache. She knew then that part of her had just died and that she would never recover. All was lost.

In that moment though, one tiny shred of hope appeared in her malfunctioning brain. Before she shut down completely, she thought of Jessie. She wasn't in her bed. She must be alive!

Wendy ran from the room, arms out in front of her, desperate. She looked like a deranged animal. But like any animal or human, a mother would do anything to protect their child, even when there is hardly any hope.

She burst into Jessie's room and double checked everything.

She was elated to see no blood, anywhere.

She checked the den. She hungrily devoured the room, her only function... her only purpose was to find her daughter, unharmed. She threw cushions in her wake and knocked the coffee table over - she didn't care... nothing else mattered now.

With a yell of frustration, she shot out of the room, like a scolded cat.

She opened the last door and stopped dead.

The windowless bathroom was dimly lit. Several small candles were glowing brightly, their flickering, eerie orange flames casting shadows around the small room. The candles had been placed strategically, almost methodically. Together, they provided sufficient light for Wendy to see. What she saw was ingrained... if not branded on to her retinas, then and there, for all eternity.

Kathy sat cross legged on the tiled floor. She had her head down. She was soaked... as was the whole floor it seemed.

Wendy could not tear her eyes away to look anywhere else but at the horror that she was witnessing right in front of her. She could feel the soggy carpet under her shoes, where the water from the bathroom had clearly seeped under the door.

Kathy continued to sit motionless. She did not react to Wendy's presence. She did not move, not one muscle... except her left arm.

She was methodically moving it, in a stroking motion.

What she was stroking, was Wendy's youngest daughter's head.

Jessie lay in the bath, fully clothed. Her eyes were shut, and she looked like she was peacefully sleeping.

The bath was unusually full and only Jessie's head was breaking the surface.

Kathy continued to stroke the top of Jessie's head, her wet matted blond hair not moving with the motion.

Suddenly Kathy stopped the rhythmic motion and turned sharply to look up at Wendy.

She stared at her blankly, with no emotion. Her eyes were large in the dimly lit room. They seemed not to be Kathy's, Wendy thought as she raised a hand to her mouth in utter horror. They seemed dead... as if Kathy was no longer in there.

She truly had gone insane.

The moment Wendy moved an inch towards her dead daughter; Kathy was up in a flash. Before Wendy could utter a word or raise a hand in defence, a powerful arm swung at her.

The bunched-up fist hit Wendy in the face with such velocity, she fell back smashing her head into the wall. She passed out cold, then and there…almost within arm's reach of her youngest daughter, her daughter who would never open her eyes again.

Wendy lay there still. She had remembered everything. The pain she felt in her chest, in her heart specifically, was inexplicable.

Wendy truly had lost everything. Whatever hell she was now entombed in was just the finale of one, catastrophic nightmare.

She closed her eyes, wishing… hoping for death to take her quickly.

Suddenly, a noise froze her thoughts. She opened her eyes staring up in the pitch blackness.

It was the surface above her. It was making an odd noise. It was… creaking. To Wendy's utter astonishment, the hard surface mere inches above her face, began to move! It was being lifted… opened!

A split second later, Wendy was staring up at the moon light. Fresh air filled her lungs. The fowl smelling stuff she had been breathing was pushed out forcefully with relief.

She didn't move though. She couldn't of course as she was bound… but she didn't even try to.

Stood several feet above her, was Kathy. She stared down at her with those dead eyes… no emotion… no discernible features even.

She screamed, but little to no noise escaped her taped lips.

Suddenly, Wendy made the mistake of looking from Kathy to her surroundings. It was then that she realised, she was not going to survive this.

She was in a grave. six feet down perhaps. The hard, solid item, taken off her was the lid to a coffin. She craned her neck left to try to look behind her… below her.

To her absolute horror and disgust, she was laying atop a dead body.

It had once been a woman it seemed by the long hair. She was elderly and had begun to decompose. Her skin was falling off her bones. This was clearly where the smell had been coming from.

Although she must have been embalmed... she was clearly not a 'fresh' corpse and therefore this had made the smell... and even worse... the adequate space for Wendy.

She threw up then, in her mouth. With no exit, she began to choke. She could not breathe. Her eyes bulged and she tried to raise her hands.

Kathy didn't move... she didn't say anything. She just stared down at Wendy.

The last thing that Wendy remembered, before darkness and the sweet release of death took her, was Kathy saying one simple sentence.

'The voices... they told me you all must die, for everyone else to live.'

As her eyes glazed over and the life left her body, the darkness returned. Kathy had placed the lid to the coffin back in its rightful place and began to cover it with the freshly dug earth, that she had removed a mere hour before.

CHAPTER 21

Wendy dabbed at her eyes with a rather worn-out looking hanky. Jonny just sat there. He had an empathetic smile across his lips and a somewhat worried frown upon his features.

'I am so sorry, Wendy,' Jonny began. 'If I had known... I would have never expected you to share that... its truly awful... I am deeply sorry,' he finished, quietly.

Wendy just stared at the hanky for several moments, and then looked up at Jonny.

She smiled sadly and said, 'It feels good to discuss it, Jonny, thank you for listening. I've had it rough, sure... but now I get to see my girls regularly, and its everything I could have wished for,' She said dreamily.

Jonny bit his lip. He felt selfish, but the first thing that crossed his mind after this statement by Wendy, was that he had only just started his time here. His sentence. He didn't even know how long he had to be here for, what a blow!

He mentally chided himself for being so inconsiderate and reminded himself that he was in the 'green section'... a short amount of time, apparently.

Also, he had to remind himself that as long as he made an effort with this place... he would feel like he had hardly been here at all! Not to mention there was one massive win with all of this... a blessing in disguise of the biggest sort; Autumn was here. What are the odds! Even Wendy thought it was crazy how lucky Jonny had got with that!

Jonny sighed and sat back in his chair. He smiled, took a sip of Bourbon and asked the question that had been burning his insides for the last few minutes like supercharged curry.

'Is it... awesome?' Wendy looked at him for a long while... slowly a big grin crept onto her face.

'It's everything you could want, hun. You'll love it. Whatta way to spend eternity,' she said, still smiling.

Jonny thought for a moment and then asked suddenly, 'Whilst you're working... do you just stay here the whole time?'

'No, no, I'm allowed through that door,' she said, pointing at the door behind her, that Bob had entered and exited earlier. 'You're not though, so don't ever try it... that would be a shitstorm, trust me!' she said, the last part, almost a scold.

'I go out to drop information at Bob's desk... meet other colleagues, who do a similar job to me... usually around the water cooler... stereotypical I know!' she said, laughing.

Jonny raised his hand like a school child. He did this for comic effect, but he did genuinely have another question.

'Question,' he said simply, with a smile.

Wendy rolled her eyes at his attempt at humour. 'What a surprise!' she said sarcastically.

'What happens if someone... kicks off?' Jonny said slowly, as if he was trying to think of the right way to ask the question.

Wendy smiled. 'You gonna get lippy with me, babe?' she asked with a laugh.

'No way!' Jonny said with a laugh, his hands raised in defence.

Wendy smirked and opened a drawer on the left side of her desk. She reached in and pulled out an old landline phone. She banged it down on the table... it was clearly heavy. It's bells clanged slightly as she did this.

It was an old rotary dial telephone, and it was London bus red.

'Wow!' Jonny exclaimed. 'You get all the latest tech,

Wend!' he continued sarcastically, with a grin.

Wendy chuckled. 'You know what really doesn't help? We find out from our patrons and our colleagues... not to mention the files and the computer system... exactly what's going on in the mortal world! That means I know all about the damn iPhone and even Sabrina Carpenter!' She laughed as she said this, but Jonny could sense more than a hint of bitterness in the comment.

'You haven't missed much, Wend,' he said, trying to lighten the mood.

She just simply nodded a few times and picked up her mug. Before taking another swig of the liquid, she stared at the mug itself. She smiled and stroked the letters on the front, 'Best Mom'.

She looked back at him and said, 'The phone connects straight to Bob, who would come and assist... or bring some muscle with him. Luckily, we can't get hurt here... so that's a bonus.'

'Cool! So, I can go burn my hand on the cook's stove then?' Jonny asked with a laugh.

'Sure!' Wendy said with a smirk. 'But I think you'd be in a lot of pain,' she continued, matter-of-factly.

'Huh?' was all Jonny could say; a picture of confusion across his features.

Wendy laughed. 'This is Purgatory, babe!' Her eyebrows were raised high, and she slapped her hands down on the table.

'It won't *hurt* you... as in you won't die or anything... but you'll sure feel pain! Trust me!' she chuckled.

Jonny was slightly deflated from that. He slunk back in his chair and sighed.

'By the way...' Wendy began, clearly not fussed about

Jonny's now less than happy demeanour. 'I'm pretty sure my Paradise break is coming up soon... so you'll have someone else here covering for me. Don't ask me who... its usually someone different every time,' she finished, tiredly.

Suddenly the door into the diner flew open. Jonny and Wendy both jumped a foot off their seats. Ray was stood there; panic ebbed across his features. He was sweating profusely and looked extremely worried.

Wendy's face was a picture of frustration, Jonny noticed... but it changed almost immediately after seeing Ray's manner.

Wendy stood up, worry now creasing her brow. 'What is it, Ray?' she asked, quietly but firmly.

'G...Georgia,' he stuttered. 'Georgia... the bride... she just left the diner!'

CHAPTER 22

Everything was suddenly going a million miles an hour, Jonny thought.

Wendy had shot up, grabbed the red telephone's handset, stabbed a number and sharply said 'Exit, exit, exit.' She had then flung the handset back down on the cradle, making the bells inside the old telephone jingle.

She had then stormed out of the office, into the diner, quickly followed by Ray, on her heals.

Before Jonny had even fully stood from his seat, the door at the back of the office had flown open and a dishevelled, sweaty Bob had appeared. He hadn't even looked at Jonny. He just marched over to the diner's door and walked through.

Jonny hesitated as he didn't really know what to do.

Should he stay here and wait? Perhaps snoop around?

Should he go crazy and go through the back door even?

He decided to slowly approach the door back into the diner.

It was fairly quiet in the diner, Jonny noticed, as he stood by the bathroom door, surveying the restaurant.

There were worried murmurs all around the room. People looked scared... surprised even, if not downright shocked. The juke box sat silent in the corner and no staff bustled around the tables. They were all crowded around Wendy at the front of the diner.

Jonny could make out Wendy, Ray, Frankie and Bob. There were a couple of others there too that he didn't know but had seen waiting tables in the diner or sweeping the floor. Two were women and one was a fairly elderly man.

He could only see the backs of Wendy, Ray and Frankie,

but Bob was facing Wendy, which meant he was facing the diner. Jonny could see the serious and almost scared look on Bob's face, even from the back of the diner. His hand kept going to his head, where he wiped his brow, or fussed with his glasses, almost like a tick or habit.

Jonny slowly began to make his way down the aisle, back towards his booth.

Autumn was still sat there, her neck stretched outwards so she could get a glimpse at what was going on at the front of the diner.

He made it back and slid onto the bench so that he was facing Autumn.

She jumped slightly in surprise, clearly engrossed in staring at what was going on with Wendy and the others.

Her pretty features were a mask of concern and worry. Tears seemed almost ready to fall from her large green eyes, somehow making them even more beautiful... more bewitching.

She focused on Jonny then and gave the smallest of smiles, it did not manage to make it to her eyes though.

'What's going on, Autumn?' Jonny asked, although he had a pretty good idea.

'She... she just walked out, Jonny!' Autumn said shrilly, the tears beginning to break through the barrier of her faux steadiness.

'OK.' Jonny said reassuringly and comfortingly. 'Tell me exactly what happened, babe,' he continued, quietly.

Autumn didn't say anything for a long moment. She had gone back to staring at the crowd of people, by the diner's entrance.

Jonny turned in his seat to have a look himself. Nothing had really changed, so he turned back round to focus on

Autumn.

He took her hand, which seemed to be shaking slightly. It was soft but cool and slightly damp to the touch. Autumn was clearly very upset, he thought.

'Come on, babe, tell me... I might be able to help or at least fill in some gaps,' he stated.

Autumn focused on him then, placing her other hand on top of his, making it a sandwich.

'Georgia was chatting to that asshole at the diner's bar, and then she got up and walked over to the door! Without hesitation... she walked right through. Not another word to anyone! My God!' Autumn said, beginning to cry. The last words were just a choked whisper.

'OK, OK,' Jonny said, trying to calm Autumn down. 'How long did they speak for?' he continued, softly.

'I dunno, Jonny... fifteen or twenty minutes maybe,' she murmured, still clearly distressed.

'Did she look upset or angry or... I dunno, anything?' Jonny said, frustration laced his words ever so slightly.

'No, no!' Autumn said, her voice slightly raising again. 'She... she looked stoic almost!' She said, a hint of hysteria in her voice and a confused expression furrowed her delicate eyebrows.

'Sshh,' Jonny cooed. 'It's OK lovely, just take a few breaths and tell me in your own time.'

Autumn did as Jonny asked and clearly appreciated the soft, gentle voice. Jonny also knew how to speak to Autumn. She was a level-headed individual; she always had been, but he knew she was too good... too trusting sometimes.

She didn't get upset easily, but it had happened several times, during their relationship. It was usually over something such as miscommunication from someone, which had caused an issue for others...or someone thinking she must be a bitch because she was pretty and had a fairly carefree, happy outlook on life.

Jonny had always felt his heart ache for her in situations like that because he truly knew, she didn't have a bad bone in her body. He also felt protective of her. Not in a jealous way but simply the fact that he loved her, knew she was an awesome person, and she didn't have any big brothers to weigh in for her.

Autumn took another deep breath and then gave a small smile.

'Thank you, babe,' she said quietly. 'You always know the right thing to say to me,' she continued, the smile growing a little more.

'It's OK, hun, just take your time and tell me anything else that you think may be relevant,' Jonny said quietly, almost cautiously.

He looked around then, he felt he needed to ensure they were not being watched or listened to. It felt conspiratorial.

A sigh of relief escaped his lips almost silently. He was confident that they were indeed being ignored by everyone.

'Before she spoke to Bear, she had spoken to Ray at the booth she was sat at. I assume they were gossiping and ordering a drink or something,' Autumn said finally, briefly pointing to an empty booth halfway across the other side of the diner.

'After that, she went to the ladies. She was in there a little while I think... but I wasn't really paying attention, Jonny,' she said, the last bit almost defensive.

'It's OK, babe... why would you watch someone for no reason? You didn't know she would do what she did,' Jonny said reassuringly.

It seemed to help too. Autumn seemed to relax into the seat somewhat, rather than sitting ram rod straight as she had been, when he had arrived back at the booth.

'I didn't see her leave the bathroom to be honest... I just noticed her approach Bear, sit on the stool next to him and speak to him for some time,' she continued.

'It seemed to be a fairly serious conversation as they were both leaning into each other, concentrating. It's the only reason I really noticed her, to be honest,' she said thoughtfully.

Jonny thought about this, he ran a hand through his medium length, wavey hair.

'So?' Jonny queried, delicately. 'She could have spoken to someone else in the loo or perhaps when you didn't see her... the loos are behind you after all,' he continued. This came out more as a theory than anything else. He was being thoughtful and trying to use his brain to the best of his ability. He felt like he needed to help with this situation.

Autumn, clearly thought about this, a frown deep on her brow. She focused on him then and said 'Yeah, you're right, Jonny, it could have been someone in the bathroom... but who?' she questioned, thoughtfully.

'I dunno,' Jonny said, honestly. He was about to say more, but Autumn straightened again in her seat. She was staring behind Jonny, over at the diner's entrance. Her eyes were a little wider, she seemed almost expectant.

At this, Jonny decided to turn and look at what Autumn had seen.

As he did, he noticed the crowd of staff had dispersed from the entrance to the diner.

Wendy now stood arms crossed, her back to the door. Her face was a mask of seriousness and underlying fury.

Bob stood next to her. He had removed his glasses and was

wiping them on his shirt. Although he towered over Wendy with his thin, lanky form... in her presence... he seemed to be dwarfed by her persona.

Bob seemed shy and reluctant, but he spoke regardless.

The wind had picked up and was howling more than ever as Bob tried to speak. The rain was relentless also – it hammered down on the windowpanes. Jonny feared one may even crack, or at the very least, leak.

Bob cleared his throat and went to try again. Before he could though, Wendy pushed an arm across his chest. She did not look at him, but he clearly knew this was a 'I'll do it' gesture.

'Georgia has left us,' she stated, clear and loudly.

The diner was silent as everyone listened, hanging on every word.

'She walked out that door,' Wendy continued; a thumb pointing behind her.

'We have no idea why this has happened. Georgia was a messed-up kid, I'll admit... but this was... unexpected,' Wendy said... the last word slower like she was contemplating her words; being careful.

'Everyone here has the right to leave, as you know,' she began again.

'But we highly advise you do *not*. Everyone knows this, as did Georgia,' she continued.

Wendy paused then. She took her time to look around the diner, her eyes falling on a few patrons, especially Bear... her gaze lingering on him the longest.

When she spoke again, a chill ran down Jonny's spine... he guessed the seriousness of situation had hit him all at once.

'I will only say this once,' she said matter-of-factly.

'We do not judge here. We do not extend your stay here if

you piss someone else off. We do not even have the ability to force you through that damn door.' She continued, her voice rising, anger almost overflowing.

'But...' She paused, seemingly for effect.

'*You* do not have the right to force anyone out of here...

If I find out that someone purposefully convinced Georgia to leave... I will report this to Bob... and he will see (as this is extremely unusual circumstances) if anything can be done about it. Understood?' she finished, her eyebrows raised, as if to challenge anyone to speak up. No one dared.

With that, Wendy stormed off towards her office, closely followed by Bob.

The door slammed and everyone looked around quizzically.

Slowly, the diner began to turn back to normal. The noise level began to rise, the staff started moving around again to the various patrons... even the juke box started up again. It played a soulful, sad tune from the sixties that seemed to fit the mood perfectly.

Jonny was about to start talking to Autumn about his time with Wendy, when he stopped. Out of the corner of his eye, he noticed the scruffy looking teenager, stand up from the stool on the other side of Bear. She walked round so that she was facing his back.

He clearly felt the presence behind him and turned to face her. Bear's face had a lop sided, shit eating grin on it.

Jonny could not see much of the teenager as her back was to him, and her hood was up around her head. To his utter shock though, in what seemed almost slow motion - she picked up her skateboard and smashed it round the side of Bear's head.

CHAPTER 23

Bear reeled from the blow. His face conveyed shock, which quickly turned to unbridled anger.

With catlike reflexes, he grabbed the skateboard as it began its second swing towards his head.

He pushed the girl hard. She fell down onto her rump, her face a picture of masked fear.

The diner had once again gone quiet, not silent... just whispers could be heard, like the trees shedding their leaves in the fall.

People were standing too. Some clearly just wanted a better view. Jonny assumed these people were the ones who had been here the longest, and any type of action was worth getting front row seats for.

The others that stood had concerned looks on their faces. Some held hands to their mouths, one person even put both hands over their eyes.

Jonny noticed the chef, Frankie, was shouting now at Bear, telling him to calm down and leave her alone.

Bear wasn't listening though. He was enraged, clearly. Just as the girl began to stand (using one of the diner's stools for leverage), he grabbed the teen by her hair. He roughly began to pull her down the aisle of the diner.

With dawning horror, Jonny realised what he was doing. He was heading for the exit...the gateway to Hell.

Jonny wasn't one for fights. He was a confident enough guy but always tended to get on with everyone. People liked him, he was an easy guy to befriend. Jonny felt he was more of a lover then a fighter.

Saying that Jonny was well built and strong. He had only

really had to throw his weight around a few times.

Excluding the tragic fuel station fight; only one memory clearly came to mind where he had to get into a real fight with someone.

Jonny had always been, and still was a real believer in fairness. He strongly believed men and women were equally made and therefore deserved to be treated equally.

If he was honest, he tended to think that women got the edge for being the superior and better sex... they generally tended to be better people, he felt.

That's why, one night when he was coming back from a dorm party at university, he stepped into a situation that had nothing to do with him.

He had been fairly well lubricated from a variety of drinking games that night. He was in a fairly decent mood, although he was a little pissed that he had to walk back alone. All his friends had decided to hook up with girls, and he wasn't feeling the vibe that night.

He had come across a couple. Initially he thought they were embracing but as he got closer, he noticed the raised voices and the fact that the taller figure was holding on to the smaller figure's wrists. As he approached them, he could see the girl was slight, perhaps only just over five foot. She had long dark hair and was crying. Her eyes were deep rimmed with mascara. Lines ran down her face like black rivers.

The man was skinny, but at least a foot taller than her.

As Jonny became level with them, the man turned to look at Jonny. He was baring his teeth like an animal. He looked at Jonny with undisguised hatred. He was clearly loaded, perhaps even high, Jonny thought.

'Keep on walking pal, this ain't nothing to do with you,' the guy had said in a low rumble of a voice, clearly trying to sound as bolshie as possible. It was menacing though, and Jonny wasn't comfortable leaving the girl with him.

She was looking at Jonny with pleading eyes. Then she did something that sealed the deal for Jonny. She mouthed the word, 'Help'.

Jonny moved in then. He decided to try the friendly tact, first of all. 'Leave it, dude, it isn't worth it. Go home and sleep it off.'

This sadly seemed to just aggravate the guy more. His eyes were wide, his pupils clearly dilated. Jonny's assumptions about what he had been up to that night, seemed to be correct.

He let go of the girl's wrists then and approached Jonny. He was breathing hard, almost as if he was trying to pump himself up.

As the guy stood nose to nose with Jonny, his eyes gave away that he wasn't as confident about the situation, as he'd like Jonny to think he was. The guy had clearly underestimated Jonny's bulk and was now probably regretting it.

Saying that, he still squared up to Jonny. These types of men will never back down, Jonny thought; especially if they don't want to be shown up in front of someone... even worse if it is a girl.

'You want some, pal?' the guy said right in Jonny's face, his cheeks flushed red with anger. Spittle hit Jonny's face as he spoke. He wiped his face slowly with the arm of his hoodie and took a small step back.

The guy looked delighted, and some stronger fake bravado came to his face and voice. 'Yeah, that's right... move on, pussy!'

The problem was, in the guy's delirious and inebriated state, he hadn't realised that Jonny had purposely moved back to get a better position.

In a sudden vicious blow, Jonny brought his head down hard and fast, smashing into the other guy's forehead and nose.

His nose erupted with blood. His hands flew up to his nose, which he cradled and began to whimper. 'You broke my nose, you fucking nutcase!' he shouted in a high-pitched voice. His demeanour had changed significantly.

Jonny ignored him, looked past the bloody mess and eyed the girl, concern showing on his features. 'Are you OK?' he asked her.

The girl nodded quickly and then said, 'thank you'.

Due to the intoxicated state of her asshole date or whatever he was, he then decided he wasn't done. The alcohol gave him balls; Jonny had to admit.

With a quick few jabs, the guy struck Jonny in the chest and then the chin.

Jonny wasn't taken aback exactly, yet he was still a little surprised at the precision of the clearly wasted mess of a man in front of him.

The guy was grinning now, thinking he had the upper hand.

Jonny touched his chin and then made a nonchalant sort of face at the guy. This enraged him as Jonny expected. The guy came for him again. This time Jonny was ready. He caught him with a right hook, right on the cheekbone. Jonny felt some mild satisfaction as he felt something give in his opponent's jaw.

The guy cried out and stumbled, then fell. He kicked out at Jonny, brushing his shin. He had to give him credit... even in what must have been total agony, he still tried to fight again.

Jonny would have let it go if it wasn't for the guy's next word. 'Bitch!' he screamed at the girl, who began to run away, her heels clicking loudly on the tarmac.

Jonny gave him a swift kick in the ribs for that which made him ball up in the foetal position.

Jonny got down on one knee then. His anger was beginning to get the better of him and he tried to keep his cool.

He leant close to the guy's ear, grabbed it hard and spoke quietly and calmly into it.

'Listen, you little prick. If you ever touch her again... if you ever act like that around any woman again... I will put you in a coma. You think this is bad? You haven't seen anything yet. Do not let me have this conversation with you again, OK?'

The guy didn't answer at first, so Jonny twisted his ear and grabbed his broken jaw with his spare hand. The guy screamed in agony.

'OK, OK!' he screamed, pleading.

Jonny pushed his face away roughly, stood up and walked away, leaving the guy to cry on his own. It began to rain then. Karma's a bitch, Jonny thought.

Jonny shook away the thoughts of the past, as quickly as they had come to him, the situation in front of him was far to serious. They continued to watch in horror for a few more seconds, as Bear pulled the girl, by her hair towards the front of the diner. Her legs were kicking out, flailing. She yelled obscenities all the way.

Jonny stood then. He couldn't just watch this happen. If no one else was going to help, he would.

Autumn did not try to stop him, although her face was a mask of concern. Jonny began to march towards the pair, hoping to intercept them.

As he did, he noticed Frankie come out from the kitchen, he was storming up behind them with a frying pan in his hand. He looked angry and ready for a fight.

They both met the pair, a mere meter from the door.

Bear stopped when he noticed the two men. He looked at Frankie and then turned slowly to look at Jonny. He was grinning. He wanted this, Jonny thought.

He let go of the girl's hair and she scooted out of reach, tears now rolling down her face. She awkwardly stood up using both her hands and ran towards the back of the diner. Jonny noticed Autumn stand and move quickly after her. Just then the manager's door flew open and both Wendy and Bob appeared.

It all happened so quickly; Jonny didn't even know at first that he had been hurt. Then the pain began to seep into his mind, and he realised.

He looked down, there was a steak knife sticking out of his thigh. Whilst looking at Autumn and then Wendy and Bob, Bear had taken advantage of the distraction and had stabbed Jonny.

Blood seeped through his jeans quickly. Frankie noticed a split second after Jonny and he went for Bear. He slammed his frying pan into the side of Bears head. The blow seemed to hit its target successfully as Bear gave a loud grunt and went to one knee.

In one unbelievable move that momentarily stunned Jonny, Bear grabbed the knife handle and yanked it from Jonny's thigh.

Without hesitation, he swiftly slashed it across Frankie's stomach. His greasy white apron split, and blood poured all over both the apron and the floor.

Frankie was in utter shock. He dropped the frying pan and brought his hands to his stomach. He fell to his knees and held onto a table to stop himself going down onto his back.

Wendy and Bob began to run towards the commotion.

Bear looked like a cornered animal. His eyes were wide,

and he was foaming at the mouth. His lips were drawn back in a vicious snarl. He had regained his footing by then and stared and Jonny, wildly.

Jonny stepped forward quickly and grabbed his leather jacket with one hand. With a balled-up fist in the other, he struck Bear under the chin.

Jonny had hit him as hard as he could muster. Bear flew back; his head cracked against the glass window. He slid down to the floor, looking fairly deflated.

Everyone, including Wendy and Bob began to crowd around both of them, to ensure they were OK. Obviously, they were not mortally wounded, Jonny knew that, but he was still in great pain. He also knew that Frankie must have been in agony.

Suddenly, to everyone's surprise, the bell above the diner's door jangled.

Everyone went silent. Even the injured Jonny and Frankie. They all turned to look at the door.

It was open. Bear stood in the doorway, looking out into the howling night. The weather was horrendous. It was worse than Jonny had seen yet. It seemed to enter the diner. Napkins and bits of paper floated around the room in the breeze, almost like a vortex was being created.

Bear turned then to look at them. He had a stoic look on his face and a lop-sided grin, once again.

'I can't be doing with all of you pussies anymore!' he shouted over the thrashing rain and wind.

'You all think I'm the Devil, right? Well, you're all welcome! I'm going home you bunch of piss-stained parasites!' he continued, almost in a scream.

Thunder crashed over them suddenly, and to everyone's utter shock, Bear walked out into the all-consuming night.

CHAPTER 24

Jonny felt sick. He put a hand to his thigh gingerly and touched the freshly dressed wound. It still stung but surprisingly, the pain was beginning to ebb fairly quickly.

He looked around the diner. Haunted faces stared at one another. His own haunted face looked around and settled on Frankie.

Similar to Jonny, Frankie had been bandaged up and was now half lying, half sitting in a booth.

Everyone was looking around and the buzz of anticipation was palpable.

Now that everything and everyone was cleaned up, Wendy was going to say something... a statement of some kind, Jonny presumed.

'This is to do with down there,' Autumn said to him, pointing down, conspiratorially.

They were now sat back in their booth. They held hands. Not necessarily out of love or desire, but out of need and want. That night (however long it was) had been a shocker for everyone. Especially Jonny, who had joined so recently. The newest recruit, he thought to himself, bitterly.

'What do you mean?' Jonny asked her quietly, still looking around.

Autumn looked around cautiously before she spoke. When she did it was barely above a whisper. 'I've heard rumours that the gatekeeper for down there...' She pointed down once again, 'is here... in this sector... perhaps even this very diner!' She was animated now, clearly scared but also excited to share this piece of information with someone.

'Who else knows?' Jonny queried.

'I don't know to be honest... I've only discussed it with Ray who hears whisperings from behind the scenes... I don't think he tells just anyone though,' Autumn replied, thoughtfully.

'OK,' Jonny said with a furrowed brow. 'So... this gatekeeper... are we talking about *the Devil*?' he continued, in just a whisper.

Autumn didn't say anything, she just nodded slowly at him; childlike almost... like a five-year-old would if you asked if the dog really ate their homework.

Jonny let out a long, slow breath. He looked at her, eyebrows raised.

'Shit,' was all he said. Then his mind wondered back to the office, when Bob appeared and was going on about confirmation of something...something in this sector. Realisation dawned on his face, and he looked intently at Autumn.

'When I was in the office, Bob came out and said something like "it's been confirmed for this sector," that must be about the same thing, right?' he asked, running his hand, thoughtfully over his beard.

Autumn's eyes were wide; her mouth open a little in the shape of a small O.

'Yeah, it must be Jonny... Jesus, this is crazy!' she hissed.

Before they could say anything else, Wendy came marching out of her office, again followed closely by Bob. He had to almost jog to keep up with her.

They headed for the centre of the diner. Everyone went quiet. She stood onto a chair (provided by one of the staff that Jonny didn't know yet) and then onto one of the booth tables. She could clearly see everyone now and they could see her.

Jonny stared over, noticing even Bob was looking up at

her.

She looked around slowly to check everyone was focused on her, it seemed.

She clearly wanted everyone's undivided attention.

She took a deep breath and began. 'Hey everyone, thank you for your patience. I appreciate it's been a crazy night... different to what we are all used to.'

She took a breath, seeming to gather her thoughts and then continued, 'As you know, we have lost two patrons this evening. This is very sad but there is *nothing* we can do about it, OK?'

She looked around at this point, waiting to see if anyone would challenge her. They did not. They all looked down, mournfully so, including Jonny.

'Bob and I have something important to report also,' she continued.

She looked at Bob for affirmation before continuing. He nodded.

'The gatekeeper of below... the Devil if you prefer... he is in Purgatory. It has been confirmed that he is within this very sector... obviously he is not meant to be, and it is very serious... however, I do not think this is a cause for concern or panic, OK?' she said, firmly.

I do not *know* if he is within this very diner or somewhere else in the sector. Bob and I have discussed this in detail, and we think there is a good chance that it was indeed Bear. If this is the case, we have nothing to worry about whatsoever,' she continued.

'Umm... what if it's not Bear, Wendy?' A short, chunky woman asked in a German sounding accent.

'There is still no cause for concern everyone,' she replied. 'We just have to be cautious and careful, OK? That is all...

trust me,' she continued. Jonny thought he could see concern or was it fear in her eyes... he couldn't be sure though.

Jonny spoke up then. He did so suddenly and loudly to get everyone's attention. An important question had crossed his mind, and he just had to get an answer.

'Wendy? Sorry... I'm new here, but... if *the Devil* is here... what the hell is going on down there?' He pointed to the ground.

Wendy rolled her eyes and looked at him in exasperation.

'Jonny. As I explained to you earlier, this is another plane of existence, OK? The big wigs around here are not former humans like us... they can do an endless amount of things that would shock and awe you, yeah? Remember... who are we to question the cosmos, right?' she said defiantly.

Before Jonny could say anything, Wendy continued, 'The gatekeeper... or the Devil (if you will), can be in numerous places at once. If he is here, he is still down there, running the show. OK?' The last bit was a statement, not a question.

Before anyone else could ask any more questions, Wendy simply said, 'We will keep you posted... do not worry, just be vigilant. Thank you.'

With that she got down quickly and headed back to her office, Bob following slower this time. He looked around as he went back to the office, almost apologetically smiling at those who made eye contact with him.

Jonny and Autumn just stared at each other... both in shock... neither knowing what to say, it seemed.

It turned out, neither needed to worry, as it was Ray who spoke next.

He appeared next to them, almost hovering. He bent down so that he was eye level and raised his eyebrows at Autumn.

'See, I fucking knew it!' he hissed, then looked around

conspiratorially.

Both Autumn and Jonny simply nodded their heads in agreement.

'You filled Jonny in then?' Ray asked Autumn, no annoyance in his voice, he almost seemed glad that she had shared this information.

Autumn nodded again and Ray smiled at her in affirmation.

'Well, looks like he's gone anyway, so we don't need to worry boys and girls!' Ray said with a happy smile.

'You reckon it was definitely Bear then?' questioned Autumn, quietly.

'Uh, yeah! Didn't you see how that slime ball acted and what he nearly did? Crazy bastard!' Ray replied, chuckling.

'What if you're wrong?' Jonny asked seriously.

'Don't worry, I'm not! Plus, if I am... Wendy will sort all this out... you two love birds don't need to worry! Enjoy getting to know each other again! You need anything at the moment?' He asked looking at one then the other.

'No, we are good thanks, Ray.' Autumn said with a smile. Jonny nodded in agreement also.

With that, Ray sauntered off to another table.

Jonny and Autumn again just looked at each other, holding hands. They both began to smile.

'How was the interview?' Autumn asked.

'Is that what you call it? Yeah, it was OK... I can't get over the accents though. Why is everyone from... everywhere?' Jonny asked, eyebrows raised.

'Well... Wendy explained the whole, you go where you go thing, right?' Autumn queried.

'Yeah... but I assumed... I dunno, ignore me,' Jonny said, smiling but shaking his head.

'Yeah, don't worry, babe... people from all over get

put together in Purgatory. Have you noticed how we all understand each other?' She asked Jonny, a glint in her eye.

'Shit! You're right!' he exclaimed.

Autumn laughed and said, 'Just part of the magic, babe. Whatever language you speak... it doesn't matter! We all understand each other here... for us, it all sounds like English!'

Jonny flashed her a smile and chuckled.

Autumn smiled back, but somewhat shyly. With a slight quiver in her voice she said, 'You know... its incredibly lucky that we are in the same sector let alone same diner!

'I know, it is amazing!' Jonny said, smiling wide.

'I'm still in love with you, Jonny,' Autumn suddenly blurted.

He looked at her for a little while and before he could speak, she continued 'I'm sorry, I shouldn't have come out with that. I mean what if you were with someone when you died?' She shook her head, seemingly angry at herself.

'Don't be silly, Autumn... I've never stopped loving you and there was no one when I died... regardless of what's happened in-between our deaths... It's always been you, babe.

CHAPTER 25

The next days... nights... weeks, or even months... whatever it was, passed quickly.

Jonny got fully reacquainted with Autumn.

He found out, during one of their many discussions, that everyone in the diner had access to the staff room. When you entered the kitchen there were three doors. Two immediately in front of you, which lead to the kitchen itself and the second to the storeroom. The one to the left was the staff room.

It was a fairly shabby and dated room, but it was cosy, had a vending machine and no windows, thankfully.

Jonny and Autumn had visited several times up until then. Sometimes just to talk in private where they felt they could be completely honest.

Other times... to get reacquainted, physically. Being dead made no change to that. Everything worked as it should, and they both clearly still enjoyed each other's company as much.

Jonny secretly felt he had come out on top when it came to the crappy Purgatory deal.

Not only was the love of his life there with him, but she loved him still, too! Not to mention she was eighteen, absolutely perfect and just the same as she had been when she was so unfairly taken from him.

They both were genuinely happy... although they kept that to themselves as much as possible to ensure others did not comment... or worse get jealous.

Jonny had confided in Autumn that he felt he really could get through this and make the best of it – however, without her... it would ruin him. She had admitted that since he had arrived, she felt the same.

Therefore, they had made a pact to be as careful as possible, as they both did not want to rock the boat.

Every time they left the staff room and returned to the diner; Jonny had to laugh.

The archaic way they let people know that the room was 'occupied' was by locking it (of course) but also by hanging a crappy sign on the door handle saying, 'come back later'. Jonny could swear it had been swiped from some budget hotel from the nineties.

Usually when they were seated back at their booth, Ray would come over with a knowing grin. He would gossip and try to get a little information out of them about what they had been up to... or what they had discussed.

He would leave eventually, not before taking an order for a couple of shakes.

They would sit there with their shakes and just grin at each other. Jonny could feel his heart balloon with love... it was corny, but he truly felt it, he was sure.

He had to admit; he really was happier than he had been in a long time... perhaps even since Autumn had passed.

Before the funeral, Jonny had been allowed to visit Autumn. Her parents were still Catholics, so her body was placed in the church the night before, for her vigil. As her parents were not devout Catholics, they had made some amendments to the funeral, including letting Jonny visit her, alone.

He had been so afraid of seeing her. Not because the broken body of his first love was laying there in a coffin... but because once he saw her there... dead, he knew she would never return... never smile or open her eyes. That was what had terrified him.

He had gone though. He had walked up the aisle, slowly,

solemnly. A vision had appeared in his mind, like a dream. He thought of himself walking down this aisle, hand in hand with Autumn... the way things should have, no, would have been, if she had not died. The thought nearly broke him.

When he reached the open coffin and looked in, his breath caught in his throat.

She did indeed look at peace and her beauty radiated, even in death.

He placed a hand on her arm and wept. Her skin was cool to the touch, it surprised him.

Before he walked away, he placed one quick, soft kiss on her lips to say goodbye. Her lips too were cold, and this made the tears fall harder. He walked back down the aisle, not turning, not looking back.

That night, visiting Autumn... had caused nightmares for weeks after.

Just the fact that she was dead... making it real, meant he dreamt about it constantly.

The saddest thing was (and this is what always made it a nightmare in Jonny's eyes) that she never awoke, never smiled at him, never kissed him back.

It was a long time until those dreams began to fade, and some type of normalcy replaced it.

Jonny discussed this with Autumn during one of their countless chats over milkshakes.

They discussed everything, spending as much time together as possible... without (they made sure) rubbing other people's noses in it.

One of the times that they visited the staff room, they had discussed, in great detail, their experiences in the manager's office with Wendy.

This was interesting, as most of the information they had

been told, was the same. But there were other little titbits that neither knew.

For example, Autumn didn't know the full story about Wendy's horrific death. Jonny had told her the story as best he could. Autumn was shocked and appalled by what had happened to Wendy, understandably.

Autumn had told Jonny about the door that led out to the corridor and beyond.

Jonny knew they were not allowed out there, but Autumn seemed to know more.

She told him that technically anyone could go through that door, but she also explained that it would automatically set off alarms everywhere. Their alarm (in the diner) was the old fire alarm system. It would screech until the missing patron was 'apprehended'. They were always apprehended and never got further than ten feet or so into the corridor, apparently.

Autumn likened it to entering the airport in Grand Theft Auto; (which they used to play together) getting all of the wanted stars right away, she had said.

Wendy had explained to Autumn that if someone did this, it created a mountain of paperwork. One specific file in this paperwork was an automatic mandatory transfer for the unlucky bastard who had tried to leave.

Anyone who did try, was sent to a prison setting Purgatory, where they had to wait out the rest of their time... or sentence would be a more adept word. This sounded awful and Jonny was very glad to know this.

Another, much sadder story was nothing to do with Wendy, accept that she had explained it to Autumn. It was the reason why Autumn was in Purgatory.

Jonny already knew that the drunken crash had been

a major factor in the decision, but Autumn had found out (during her meeting with Wendy) there were other reasons too.

Just like Jonny, Autumn was a green, Jonny was relieved to know. Also, (just like Jonny), Autumn had been surprised and shocked at what had swung the scales in favour of Purgatory.

It was during one of these heart-to-heart visits to the staff room, that Autumn told Jonny the other reason she was in Purgatory.

CHAPTER 26
AUTUMN'S STORY

Autumn had agreed to go to the prom with Teddy. He was a nice guy, handsome and Autumn always tried to do the right thing. Usually, the right thing made her feel right; feel good even.

This didn't though... she knew in her heart that really, she wanted to go with Jonny. It was all about Jonny, the love of her life.

She had accepted Teddy's invitation as she knew she needed to go to the prom... but also, she did it to ensure Jonny noticed... and would be jealous.

Autumn was ashamed of this. Not just for affectively using Teddy but because this wasn't the type of person she was. She had never done anything like this, and she felt awful.

She had enjoyed the night, but this was thanks to spending most of it with Jonny, not with Teddy.

Afterwards, they had walked together to a coach, set up by the school for prom goers to return back to town, and get lifts from there, home.

Whilst they walked, Teddy was quiet and just stared at his feet as they walked.

'Are you OK, Teddy?' she asked.

He looked at her then, sadness and a hint of anger in his eyes. It quickly fizzled out though and he replied, 'Yeah, sure.'

They continued to walk to the coach in silence, and once they were seated halfway up, she tried again.

'I'm sorry about tonight, Teddy. I didn't mean to spend so much time chatting with Jonny,' Autumn explained.

He looked at her then and blurted, 'You... you used me, Autumn!'

Autumn looked at him, shocked, a painful expression on her soft features. Part of her was sad he felt this way, another part of her felt horrendous guilt as it was mostly true.

She lied to him then, again something she rarely did, and hated. 'No, it's not like that Teddy... you're a nice guy, I like you!'

She placed her hand on his thigh. She didn't know why she did this, but she was trying to calm him, and it was a reflex action.

She regretted it right away though, as he smiled at her, hope adorning his eyes.

She looked away and then said softly, 'I like you... but I'm not in the right place for anything at the moment, I'm sorry'.

Teddy didn't say anything for a long while. She looked at him from the corner of her eye, and noticed he was just staring at the seat in front of him, not moving. His hand was a clenched fist, and his jaw was set firm. He ran a hand through his short, close cropped black hair and then his demeanour changed back to 'normal Teddy'.

'No worries.' he said simply and began to stare out of the window, smirking to himself.

The bus pulled up to the quiet carpark mere minutes later.

Everyone got off. Autumn was one of the last to leave. As she exited the door, she noticed Teddy hadn't even got up yet.

'Off the bus, kid,' said the driver to the rear-view mirror, tiredly.

Teddy seemed to shake himself out of his revelry, he got up and marched down the aisle, a small, odd smile on his lips.

He met Autumn by the door, and they walked to a bench where they waited for their parents to collect them, individually.

They sat and watched the bus depart. It was cool that night and most people had already been collected, as their parents or rides were waiting.

Teddy stood suddenly and said, 'I need a piss, back in a sec.' He then jogged over to a building and walked down the alley beside it and disappeared from view.

Autumn sat there for a long time, nervously looking around. Eventually, she called out for Teddy but heard no answer.

She stood then, crossed the road and hesitantly walked down the alley. Her heels clicked on the tarmac, echoing between the buildings. She tried to walk softly, but it was no use.

She approached the turn where Teddy had gone and there he was, his shirt was removed, and he was just staring at her grinning wildly, almost manically. It scared Autumn to her core.

Everything made sense to her then, but not quickly enough.

Autumn turned to run but slipped in her high heels. Before she could regain her balance, Teddy was on her. He bear-hugged her and dragged her a few feet, then pressed her up against the wall, hard.

With almost demon strength, Teddy yanked her dress up high over her stockings, revealing her underwear. He viciously ripped the silky garment away in one fell swoop.

She turned to him, a pleading look in her eyes, tears running down her cheeks, making her mascara run.

'Don't do this, Teddy!' she said in a high pitch, desperate voice. Her breaths kept coming quickly, anxiety overruling her brain.

'Shut up… you little cock tease!' he spat, close to her ear. He slid his trousers down and to her horror she saw his enlarged penis sticking out of the hole in the front of his boxers.

'You think you're so perfect! Do you know how hard it's been to be 'Mr. Nice Guy' all year? Now you want to use me. I don't think so, babe…' he continued, snarling.

She did not recognise this person who now held her against her will. She cried hard and he told her to shut up otherwise he would beat her unconscious.

He began to slide his hand down her body and grabbed her buttocks, then slapped them with vicious intent. It stung and she yelped in pain. He grabbed her dark brown hair aggressively and pulled her next to his lips. 'What did I say, bitch?' he hissed, spittle hitting her cheek.

She sobbed, almost in silence. She wet herself then, pure terror making the involuntary action happen.

Teddy looked at her in disgust and spat down her cleavage. He held her closer; she could barely breathe, 'You think that's gonna stop me, twat?' he whispered into her ear.

It hit her then as she found herself in the most grotesque and shocking situation of her young life.

'I might die tonight,' she thought. Then a second thought came to her mind… firmer and stronger… 'I don't want this to happen… I *won't* let this happen!'

With that she smashed her head backwards, violently. It connected with Teddy's jaw.

He staggered back, clearly in shock and not expecting her to react.

She didn't stop there though. Before he could regain his wits, she turned and punched him right in the nose, feeling it break. Blood gushed out, almost instantly. He cried out but she couldn't stop. She continued to punch his face, his torso.

Even when he fell to one knee, she kicked and slapped at his battered body.

An evil, but to her mind, fair idea came to fruition then. She opened her purse and grabbed the can of pepper spray.

She sprayed it into his eyes. He screamed in pain, but she would not stop. She continued spraying it into his eyes until the can was empty. It felt like she was possessed.

She gave him one last kick, and he fell over, his head banging against the wall.

He passed out and she walked away, her head held high.

Just as she made it back to the bench, her parents car pulled up. She got into the front passenger seat. She looked down the dark alley as they drove away, seeing nothing but the gloom of the night.

Her dad had asked how the night was and where was Teddy.

Autumn had been surprised how easily she had found it to lie to her father and even fake a smile. She made out like it had been a wonderful night and that Teddy had bumped into some friends that she didn't know, and asked if it was OK to leave with them. She said she had agreed as she knew her dad would pick her up shortly.

Autumn never reported it, both the attempted rape and the vicious beating she had given Teddy.

Autumn had gone to bed that night after a burning hot shower. She made a pact with herself that she would forget this, never speak of it to anyone and *not* let it affect her life for one moment.

She had upheld this pact until her untimely death. Even when Teddy was found early the next morning. Someone who worked in a warehouse round the back of those buildings had found him, awake but disoriented.

Even when it was reported all over the school that the nice guy, Teddy had been attacked and was now all but blind from his injuries and would be pissing into a bag for the rest of his life.

Even when the police questioned her, as he was her date at the prom.

Even when Jonny had asked what happened.

She kept the pact the whole time. No one ever thought she had done anything and likewise, no one thought that 'Mr. Nice Guy, Teddy' would ever hurt anyone...

It was deemed a malicious, unprovoked attack and it quickly ended in the pages of history.

Teddy never spoke to Autumn again and she had never spoken to him.

She avoided him the few times that she saw him in the hallways of their school, white stick in hand.

Teddy was clearly struggling though; people began to notice. He could no longer do sports... which was what he was best at. Autumn felt no remorse though and certainly no sorrow for Teddy.

After a few weeks back at school, it was clear that Teddy could not continue his education there. His parents organised for him to transfer. He quickly and quietly left the school in favour of an assisted education facility that would help with his new disabilities.

He never said anything about what really happened to a single soul. Although they had never spoken since that night, they clearly both knew that neither could. That hatred had created a bond... a secret... that would never be spoken of.

Autumn really did manage to virtually forget the incident. She continued to be the person she had always been and was proud of herself for maintaining this.

Although she never regretted her actions; she was subconsciously surprised at what any person could do if they found themselves in a 'kill or be killed' type scenario.

After all, they say we only use ten percent of our brain, she often mused.

Although she compartmentalised all of this, the one thing that would sometimes come to her at night, when she couldn't sleep was a cold feeling.

This feeling... or more aptly named, dread, would make her feel that someday... perhaps many decades later... she would have to pay for this in one way or another, regardless of the horrific situation in which it occurred.

CHAPTER 27

Jonny was dismayed to hear Autumn's horrific tale.

His emotions were all over the place. He was startled, in total shock, then sadness, empathy and finally anger.

'That piece of shit!' he said angrily. 'I should have known! I would have killed him! Why didn't you tell me, babe... I would have...' Jonny started ranting but was cut off by Autumn simply raising her hand. She spoke. 'You would have what, Jonny?' she asked matter-of-factly.

'I explained what happened and I also explained how I could not tell *anyone*!' she continued, eyebrows raised, a somewhat frustrated look on her features.

Jonny relaxed a little then and said, 'I'm sorry, babe, I am just really shocked by this. I mean... you know my stories and why... I am here, but this is just... It's hard to swallow is all... I mean; you don't deserve to be here!' He said, the last words almost desperate and full of emotion.

She smiled at him sadly. 'I do Jonny... sadly we all deserve to be here... that's a fact. We just have to deal with it.'

They hugged then for a long time, both had tears, and both didn't want to let go of the other, it was consoling... like they were helping each other over the past pains of life.

After that, they both felt like they needed some rest. It was strange, in Purgatory, no one really *needed* to sleep... but they did anyway. Some in booths, some in chairs, some didn't bother at all. Some took their rest in the staff room... and that is exactly what Jonny and Autumn did after Autumn had revealed all.

They rested well... Jonny thought they may have slept a little... but couldn't be sure. He felt (as he was sure Autumn did) that they knew everything about each other now and that there were no secrets. That was the way it always should have been... how it used to be. He felt good about this... it made him feel warm and content, like sticky toffee pudding made an old man feel.

When he rose, he realised he needed the bathroom badly. Autumn still seemed to be resting, so he quietly slipped out of the staff room and entered the bathroom.

The same blinking light, continued to monotonously turn on and off. He sighed, walking into a stall and relieved himself.

As he did so, he thought back to the last times he had been in here. Nothing odd had occurred since the time he passed out... or whatever it was that happened to him.

Just then, Jonny felt a chill on his neck... the hairs on his arms began to prickle and stand up. He turned slowly, as he pulled up his jeans. Nothing was there.

He sighed and slowly walked to the sink and washed his hands, staring at his reflection.

There was a bang, and all the lights went out. It was pitch black. He could not see anything. There was not a sound in the room. He noticed he couldn't even hear any faint noises from the diner.

He felt so cold... cold and afraid. It may have been black as pitch... but he could sense... he knew... that he was not alone.

He felt or sensed, someone come up close behind him. Their stinking, fetid breath was on his neck... the only thing that felt warm in the whole damn room.

Then there was a voice, speaking behind him, not much more than a whisper... but it was close to his ear, and he could hear it clearly. He could feel it too... it seemed to resonate in his very bones. The feeling was truly terrifying.

The first words the voice spoke were not actually words, they were laughter.

Once the laughter stopped, it spoke, 'You really thought I was gone? Petulant child,' it said in a sneer.

'One as powerful as I...' it continued in the same arrogant voice, 'am a master of manipulation and... to your surprise (I am sure)... I like to be honest on a regular basis!' it continued, Jonny being able to hear the smile... or grin, in its voice.

'Wh... what do you mean?' Jonny stammered.

The voice tutted slowly, feigning childlike frustration. 'I like to cause chaos my dear boy... so, I like to be honest where it suits me! They're lying to you... Wendy and that elongated streak of piss. They don't want you to know the truth,' the voice continued, a cold sensation began on both Jonny's shoulders... it felt like someone was touching him, softly.

'That's not true,' Jonny said in a shaky voice, not convincing himself, let alone the *thing* behind him.

'Ha! Please, Jonny... we both know that you're really here because you killed Autumn! You've known it since that night, all that time ago... she would have *never* been put in that situation if it wasn't for you and your dick!' it said, the last words spoken nastily and purposefully harsh.

Jonny began to sob. He could not help it. Not only was he scared out of his mind but this *thing*... spoke the truth... he felt it in his heart.

The thing feigned empathy by cooing him.

Jonny straightened then and wiped his face of fallen tears.

'Why do you care? What's in it for you?' Jonny said firmly, conjuring as much strength in his voice as he could muster.

'Oh, there's a lot of reasons I care, Jonny,' the voice said; the feeling on his shoulders now felt like he was being caressed.

'For example!' it continued in a false, cheerful voice, 'I want to make sure you're safely in the right place, Jonny. I mean... can you imagine if it turned out they lied to you, and you were in the wrong place! Preposterous! Why do a spell in Purgatory and then be told there was an 'error' and now you have to come down to my little patch of Paradise, hmm?'

Jonny thought about this, concern ate at his mind like a cancerous tumour.

Before Jonny could answer, the voice continued, in its condescending tone. 'I mean they have lied to you Jonny... I've already told you that... so what do you think that means? I'll tell you what it means... I am right... and you'll be coming down to me next!'

'No!' Jonny all but yelled. 'Once you are here, you don't get moved... that's the rules!' Jonny continued, shrilly.

'Lies and more lies,' the voice replied, nonchalantly. 'Technically you can be sent down... and you will be my friend... it's only a matter of time,' the voice said.

'So... if this is true... what would you suggest?' Jonny asked, bitterly.

'Well, it's obvious, no?' The voice answered lightly. 'You should... no you *need* to leave now and come join me! Why put it off? Plus, it's not bad down there... it's just different is all. You'll love it, I'm sure!'

Jonny was about to reply when the lights suddenly came back on, almost blinding him.

He squinted into the mirror and turned to see Frankie staring at him. 'You OK, dude?' was all that he said.

'Yeah...yeah I'm fine... just... confused, the lights all went out, and...' Jonny stopped... deciding not to say anything more.

Frankie clearly sensed that Jonny would say no more and

simply said, 'OK then.' He walked past Jonny and into the stall, closing the door.

Jonny slowly walked out of the bathroom and bumped right into Ray, who was carrying a tray ladened with over filled milkshakes.

The tray went flying, as did the shakes. They were both covered in various colours of milkshake.

'Shit! I am so sorry Ray!' Jonny said, dropping to a crouch to help pick up the plastic glasses and tray.

Ray looked exasperated and tired, but he smiled at Jonny and said, 'No harm done, Jonny. Come help me with these now dirty dishes and then we can both go get changed in the staff room.'

Jonny briefly looked over at their booth and saw that Autumn was there. She had turned round to see what the commotion was. She smiled at him and tried to hide a giggle, unsuccessfully.

Jonny grinned and rolled his eyes at her; then began to follow Ray.

They entered the kitchen and placed the now dirty dishes in the industrial dishwasher. Ray then wiped down the tray and put it on top of a stack of clean ones.

'Come on then clumsy, let's find us both some new clothes,' Ray said with a laugh.

As they walked back to the door to exit the kitchen, Jonny noticed how greasy and grimy the kitchen was. The work surfaces were clean yes, but the walls and the various appliances looked grease covered and filthy.

Ray seemed to sense this and turned to say, 'it doesn't look clean but it's safe, don't worry, hun.'

Jonny shrugged his shoulders and walked through the exit and entered the staff room, behind Ray.

'I find it weird that we don't shower, yet we don't stink, and we don't change our clothes, yet we don't feel grotty. Why is that?' Jonny questioned.

'All part of the fun, dear,' Ray answered, not looking at Jonny. He was rummaging through a cupboard next to the sofa.

'There's always clothes here for everyone who needs them. That's the magic! May not happen a lot... but sometimes we need them!' He said this with a laugh and pointed at their clothes, that were still dripping with milkshake.

'Here we go!' Ray said in a celebratory voice.

He pulled out a freshly pressed uniform for himself, and some new jeans and t-shirt for Jonny.

Both were items he owned and that he wore on a regular basis. Jonny was gob smacked.

Ray rolled his eyes and light heartedly said, 'Come on, Jonny, don't tell me stuff is still surprising you in this place?'

'Don't think it will ever stop, Ray!' Jonny answered with a laugh.

Ray laughed at this and turned to begin to change.

Jonny did the same. He removed his soaked top and smeared jeans.

'You sure had a rocket up your ass, leaving the bathroom, Jonny,' Ray said suddenly. Jonny couldn't tell if it was a statement or a question.

When Ray didn't say anything else, Jonny assumed it was a question and answered. 'Lights went out in the bathroom.'

'Anything else? I mean... I found you passed out in there one time... forgive a guy for asking,' Ray said, an overly jovial tone coming from him.

Jonny turned then to find that Ray had already done so. He was now fully clothed again and was just zipping up his trousers.

Jonny quickly put his top on and sat on the sofa with a sigh.

He placed his head in his hands and spoke. 'Something happened again in the bathroom, Ray.'

Ray came and sat next to Jonny, placing a hand on his shoulder. 'What?' was all he asked.

Jonny paused then. He was unsure if he should explain what happened. Would Ray think he was crazy? He sighed and decided to tell him, regardless.

'I heard a voice, Ray. When the lights went out... something evil spoke to me... I think it was... him,' he said breathlessly, pointing down.

Ray looked at him incredulously and said quietly, 'Jonny... it was Bear... he's gone now... you don't have anything to worry about!'

'I know, I know!' Jonny said, his voice tired and slightly irritable.

'The voice told me it wasn't Bear and that he was still here... he told me people had lied to me... he told me that Wendy had lied,' Jonny continued, his head again in his hands. He felt like he could not make eye contact with Ray whilst he explained this. He didn't want to see the reaction. Perhaps he was afraid to see, he thought.

'OK... let's say that's true... all of it... what does that mean?' Ray asked softly.

Jonny thought for a moment before answering.

'It means it's my fault that Autumn left that night, Ray. It's my fault she's dead and it's my fault she's here. I'm...' Jonny couldn't finish his sentence. He choked back a sob.

He tried again, taking a deep breath beforehand. 'I'm not meant to be here Ray. I'm meant to be down there... in hell.'

CHAPTER 28

'This is total bullshit, I'm sorry, Jonny!' Ray said theatrically.

Jonny looked up at Ray in surprise. The outburst had caught him off guard.

Ray just nodded at him, a righteous look on his face.

'Listen. The system doesn't make mistakes, and it doesn't lie, OK? Maybe your right about the damn Devil... even if he is still around, it does not mean he speaks the truth or has your best interests at heart. Believe me!' Ray said, firmly. His jovial tone a distant memory to Jonny.

'Besides,' he continued. 'You are not meant to be down there... you are meant to be here, with us...with Autumn... regardless of what has happened in the past and regardless of if this is true or that is true,' he continued, waving his hand around in a circular motion to suggest this was all just hindsight.

Jonny nodded sadly; it didn't really make him feel better, but it was nice to have someone in his corner after what he had just experienced.

Suddenly, Ray gave a short laugh and shook his head. Jonny looked at him quizzically. After a few moments, he caught Ray's eye. 'I'm sorry,' Ray started. 'It's just... you talk about people who should go... down there... well, if anyone should go down there... it's that little skater chick out there, I hear!' Ray finished, his eyes squinted, a lop-sided grin on his face.

Jonny stared at Ray, a slightly shocked expression on his features.

Ray clearly picked up on this as he added quickly, 'That's just what I've heard, mind you. Apparently not only does she deserve to go down there… but she wants to go too! I've heard that's why she was speaking to Bear. Who knows! It could have all been a set up! Sneaky little sod.'

Jonny still didn't know what to say and decided to stand up. He couldn't put his finger on it, but something about this conversation was making him feel a little awkward.

'I gotta go, Ray,' he said finally.

'No problem!' Ray said light heartedly. 'Listen though… I've been thinking about all these rumours… perhaps you should chat to the little skater girl… see why she wants to go down there… or why she deserves it?' Ray said, an eyebrow raised.

'You mean *if* she wanted to go and *if* she deserved it?' Jonny asked, incredulously.

Ray smiled at Jonny and said, 'Sorry, babe, you know me… love a bit of gossip… all of us limp wrists love a bit of bitchiness too!' He laughed and got up, strode over to the door and walked out.

Jonny was left feeling somewhat perplexed.

He didn't move for a moment and just thought about what Ray had said.

He didn't necessarily agree with Ray's words, but then again, each to their own. One thing that did make sense, however, was to speak to the girl and find out what had gone on with her and Bear.

Jonny went back to the booth then and sat with Autumn, on the same bench.

He quietly told her what had happened since he had gone to the bathroom, right up to when Ray had walked back out into the diner.

She raised her eyebrows a few times… she was clearly interested in what was going on, too.

Autumn also confided in Jonny that although she hated Bear, she didn't think he was the Devil. It seemed too easy and didn't add up. Bear made bad decisions and often rash ones. She explained to Jonny that she believed the Devil to be the ultimate manipulator. She also said he would definitely be cold and calculated. This wasn't Bear's work; she was sure of it.

After discussing it a little more, they ordered some hot dogs from Ray when he popped over to see if they needed anything.

They spoke for a little while, just general chit chat.

Before he left though, Ray did say he'd be interested to see how the chat with Becca went.

So that was her name, Jonny thought.

He also added that Jonny should be delicate with her... regardless of how hostile she might come across. The last thing Ray said before he left, was under no circumstances, should Jonny mention the rumours that Ray had told him about.

Jonny and Autumn spoke a little more after this. Once their food came, they changed the subject and tried to discuss lighter subjects.

It had been a weird night, they both agreed. They had laughed then at the absurdity of saying 'night'. It was always night here, and they both knew that wouldn't change.

After the meal, they just sat for a little while, holding hands and enjoying each other's company.

Jonny expressed his happiness once again for being with Autumn and she concurred. She looked like an angel to him, and he was damn sure he would never be without her again.

Eventually, Autumn brought up Becca again. She sighed and said, 'I think Ray's right, babe. You need to go talk to her and try to work out what has been or is going on.'

Jonny looked down for a moment and then met her eyes once again.

'Your right, hun, I need to,' he answered with a sigh of finality. His mind clearly made up.

In unison, they looked over to see what Becca was doing. She had her head down reading something at the diner's counter.

Autumn looked at Jonny and simply nodded, encouragingly.

Jonny stood on stiff legs, stretched, and began to walk towards the diner's counter.

As he passed Autumn, he placed his hand on her shoulder and gave it a little squeeze. She patted his hand, and he continued on, a purpose in his slow stride.

He hesitated a little as he approached the row of stools at the diner's counter.

No one was sat on any of them, except Becca.

He gingerly sat on the stool next to the teen. She didn't even acknowledge his presence.

He stared at her for a little while before attempting to start up a conversation. He took in her general demeanour and her baggy, skateboarder clothes. Her hood was up, but at the front he could see purple highlights just sticking out.

She was reading an old paperback, its pages yellowed by age. The spine was cracked and beginning to fall apart. Her black painted fingernails slipped under a page and turned it. The nail varnish was chipped and badly applied, perhaps on purpose, Jonny thought.

'Hey... uh, hope you don't mind if I sit here,' Jonny said cautiously.

She didn't even raise her head, let alone look at him.

'Free country... or free Purgatory, Dude,' she said in a no-

nonsense voice. Her accent clearly Scottish.

'Thanks. You're Becca, right?' Jonny quizzed.

She looked up then, eyeing him warily.

'Whose asking? You the new guy, right?' she all but demanded. Her heavily made-up eyes squinting at him incredulously. She seemed to do her best to make herself as unapproachable as possible, Jonny thought. He could see through this though. Behind the attitude and the make-up was a scared, vulnerable teen with delicate features and big, dark, pretty eyes.

'Uh yeah, I am...' Jonny replied, ignoring the first question. 'You're new too, just before me I think?' he said, making his voice as nonchalant as possible.

'Aye, for all my sins,' she replied, returning to look at her book, her voice revealing how uninterested she was in the conversation.

'Us newbies gotta stick together!' Jonny said, instantly regretting the light-hearted comment. It had 'dad vibes' written all over it. She looked at him and smirked before returning to her book. He rolled his eyes at no one and silently chided himself.

'Listen dude... I'm not up for any kinky menage a trois ideas you and your lady have,' Becca said, still looking at her book. Jonny tried to object but she continued, before he could speak. 'I may have a killer ass and could certainly do with a bit of attention... but I don't think you could get my pilot lit... if you know what I mean...'

Jonny looked confused and then realisation crossed his face. She looked at him and laughed.

'Don't worry, I won't try it on with your girl... although it is tempting,' she said, laughing again.

Jonny forced a laugh himself and tried to get on to the

subject he had come over for.

'Don't worry, I'm not here for that... I was just checking in after... after what happened,' he said cautiously.

Becca seemed to shrink a little with this comment and didn't reply.

Jonny decided to continue. 'Why the hell would he do that to you? What a jerk!'

Becca sat up then and looked at him hard. 'What do you want to know, dude? I know rumours fly around this place, so just pelt me with it, what is your deal?' she questioned, anger lacing her voice.

Jonny put his hands up in surrender. 'No, no... I'm just checking you're all good... anything you may need help with... that kind of thing,' he said apologetically.

Her features softened a little then. 'Look, don't worry... I'm fine. Anyway...' She said with a sigh, once again returning to her book.

'Don't worry about the rumours... I'm not. If anything, worry about the ones going round about you, dude,' she said.

CHAPTER 29

Jonny stared at Becca, perplexed. She once again had her head down, her nose in her book. She was acting as if Jonny didn't exist, which irritated him, somewhat. Whether she was really ignoring him or not, Jonny needed to continue speaking to her...get her to open up to him and explain what she meant.

'Becca... I need to know what you meant by that,' Jonny said simply.

She looked at him then, a smirk playing on her lips. 'It's gonna cost you, dude,' she said quietly.

Jonny began to lose his patience. 'Cut the shit, Becca. It's not really very fair is it... it's childish to be honest. It's a form of bullying which I am *not* a fan of,' he said, a warning tone in his quiet but low voice.

Something seemed to change in her demeanour then. Perhaps something he had said got through to her, Jonny thought.

She seemed to be considering her words carefully.

She rolled her eyes (clearly a false bravado lacing the expression) and said, 'The rumour is... you are in the wrong place because it's your fault that your girl over there, is here.'

Jonny swallowed a lump in his throat and paused before speaking. He didn't want to scare the girl off as she was talking to him at last.

'Where did you hear this?' he said, finally.

'Around,' she said, nonchalantly.

'There's no truth in that, Becca.' He said firmly, his knuckles going white as he balled his fists. Jonny noticed and he moved his hands under the counter, trying to act less wound up then he was.

She just shrugged her shoulders as if it didn't matter either way to her.

Jonny tried to ignore the gesture and continued speaking quietly, 'Anything else?'

She thought for a moment and then said, 'Apparently that douche, Bear, was definitely the Devil... I've been told... but... I don't buy it.'

Jonny looked at her thoughtfully and then said warily, 'I agree, and I've been told the same thing.'

Although Becca was trying to keep up her poker face, this gave her away. Her somewhat naïve, young years betrayed her in that moment.

'Really? I'm glad to hear that as no one else seems to be fussed from what I've gathered,' she said, interest glittering in her dark eyes like Christmas lights.

'So, you've spoken to other people about this then?' Jonny queried.

'No... not really... just Ray. I'm a good listener see. I've learnt over the years of dealing with bitchy girls in school, how to be unnoticed but pick up on all the titbits of information. That way I can use it to my advantage, someday, if needed, that is,' she said, a delicate but proud ghost of a smile on her lips.

Jonny couldn't help but smile at that. 'So, everyone just accepted that Bear was the Devil and now it's business as usual?' he asked incredulously.

'Aye, pretty much,' Becca replied, simply.

'Christ,' Jonny muttered under his breath.

She leaned in close to him then. He could smell the coffee on her breath. She whispered, conspiratorially, 'You haven't heard anything else then... from anyone else I mean?'

'Nope. I'm the same as you. Just what Ray has told me...

and what Autumn thinks... which is the same as me to be honest,' he replied, honestly. He rubbed at his bearded chin, confusion crossing his features.

'What is it?' Becca asked, noticing the frown on his face.

'I dunno. Probably nothing. I just feel like there's a bit of a common denominator here... you know what I mean?' He said quietly, the frown on his face, deepening.

She looked away then, cautiously checking no one was listening, it seemed to Jonny.

She leant in even closer; her eyes were slightly squinted.

'Have you had anything weird happen to you in the bathroom?' she whispered.

'Yes!' Jonny said, a little too loudly.

Becca silently cursed him for this, and he looked down, feeling like a naughty school child, caught with his pudgy little hand in the proverbial cookie jar.

'Same,' she replied thoughtfully.

Over the next few minutes, both relayed their stories of what had happened in the bathroom. Jonny explained his two odd experiences and Becca explained her single one.

Both had been told during these horrendous experiences in the bathroom, that Bear *wasn't* the Devil.

After they had swapped war stories, they just stared at each other, slightly taken aback.

'Tell me what you've heard,' Becca said deliberately slowly, in a quiet, no-nonsense tone.

'I thought you said you knew what was being said about you,' Jonny said, a challenge burning in his eyes.

'For fuck's sake, dude, yes I know there is shit going around about me but tell me first-hand what *you've* heard!' she said, a hint of desperation entering her voice.

Jonny took pity on her then. 'OK, Becca. I've heard that

you may have wanted to go... down there... that you may have even convinced Bear to help you... put on a show.' He said quietly, almost in an apologetic voice.

Anger flared in her eyes; her jaw tightened. Jonny could see the muscles flex in her throat and her cheeks flush pink with fury.

'That is total bullshit!' she hissed. 'I was talking to Bear as we had both been pitted against each other, it seemed. Apparently, there was some rumour about him, that he thought I had started and vice-versa,' Becca continued.

'That's interesting,' Jonny said quietly. 'What was the rumour?' he asked, eyebrows raised.

'Basically, it was the same for both of us... it was that we both were here by error... and that we should be... should be down there,' Becca replied, her eyes breaking contact with Jonny's, her fragile and vulnerable persona showing through for a moment.

She stared down at the floor for a while.

'That's bullshit, Becca,' Jonny said, a comforting smile on his lips.

'There are no errors. We are meant to be here. Simple as that,' He said, firmly.

In that moment, Jonny realised that he, himself had been having the same thoughts, due to these 'rumours', not because there was any basis for truth in them.

He was becoming infuriated by this fact and felt his blood pressure begin to rise.

He knew what Wendy had told him was correct. It was fair and he felt it in his soul.

He was being manipulated, he realised... and so was Becca.

'Listen, Becca. We are being fucked with here. This is manipulation,' Jonny said quietly but firmly.

She nodded her agreement and looked around cautiously.

'Look at what has happened. First Georgia, then Bear and now... well, us!' He hissed, conspiratorially.

She nodded again, her mind clearly working through this. Jonny felt his eyes had been opened to what was really going on here. The realisation of having the vail removed, was mirrored in the eyes of the girl sat next to him.

'Jonny?' Becca questioned, barely above a whisper. 'Have you been told... during all these bullshit rumours... what happened to me?'

Jonny thought this was an odd question. He simply shook his head, no.

'Has that got to do with why these rumours say you wanted to go or should have gone... down there?' he asked gingerly.

'I don't know... but that is what I'm guessing... what I'm sensing. No one should know, except Wendy... but...' Becca replied quietly, trailing off at the end.

Her eyes cast down, tears welling and beginning to fall down her cheeks.

He placed a hand on her shoulder then, trying to comfort her. He felt so angry that someone or something was doing this to them, doing this to a young girl. He gritted his teeth to stop himself yelling out in anguish.

'Becca. Will you tell me what happened to you... why you're here?' Jonny asked quietly, a quiver in his voice. He knew that if he touched a nerve or rattled this sadly damaged teen, that it could all go down the pan.

She nodded slowly, wiping tears away from her cheeks.

She looked at him then, a thought clearly coming to the forefront of her mind.

'Jonny, this *common denominator*...' She began.

Jonny cut her off, before she could speak another word, and be heard by prying ears.

'Yes,' Was all he said, a knowing look blazing in his eyes.

With that they both slowly turned and looked over to the far side of the diner.

They looked back at one another; no words passed between them... no words needed to be spoken.

They turned fully, till they were both looking into the diner's kitchen, where Frankie was busy, aggressively cleaning the stove.

Without looking away from Frankie and his chore, Jonny noticed in his peripheral vision, Becca lean sideways, so that she was close to his ear.

She whispered one word. One word that held so much weight as it connected all these tragedies together.

'Ray.'

CHAPTER 30
BECCA'S STORY

Becca was crying again, as she stripped off her sodden uniform. Her Scottish blood ran cold, as she thought back to that afternoon's lunch break in school.

She had been outed. A few girls knew before... the ones she would begrudgingly call friends.

But now everyone knew. She had fallen for Ciara when she first joined the school in the summer. A rocker chick through and through. However, she still hung out with the popular crowd – a perfect combination, Becca thought, secretly.

Becca had been smitten right away. She thought that Ciara seemed to be a genuinely nice girl. She showed great interest in Becca too. The two had become quick friends, which for a time had given Becca back some faith in humanity.

That had all changed today though. It had become instantly obvious, that it had all been a vicious game, where Becca was the toy.

Ciara had convinced Becca to go for a walk around the school grounds that lunch break. She had led her to a quiet place where students went to skip classes, smoke and make out.

Ciara had led her on by telling her she 'liked' her and that she was the same as her.

She had stroked her hair and placed a soft kiss on Becca's dark painted lips.

Becca felt like everything was falling into place for her, finally. She had grinned back at Ciara. Love was swimming in her large, dark eyes, like the waves of the ocean.

It had begun to change then, however. Ciara had asked Becca to tell her... tell her how she felt and why.

Becca, beguiled by Ciara had answered. She normally would have been extremely sceptical and run a mile... but she was drawn to this girl... like a moth to a flame.

She had confessed her love for Ciara, right then and there, blurting it out with tears of joy in her eyes.

Again, Becca had not picked up on the odd situation, when Ciara had asked, 'Why?'

Becca had answered, without hesitation. 'I'm gay!'

That had been it. Like a code word, 'gay' had made Ciara take a few steps back. A cruel smile tugging at her perfect, full lips. Becca had stared at her in confusion and then realisation and disbelief beginning to worm its way into her mind.

Previously camouflaged by foliage; students... friends of Ciara, began to appear from the bushes behind them.

Several had their mobile phones out and were filming or taking pictures. The lights of the flash searing into her eyes like lasers.

It all made sense now. The students... what felt like hundreds of them now... all laughed at her, including Ciara.

With one last violation, one sealing act, Ciara walked forwards and spat in Becca's face.

Becca howled as if in pain, her heart feeling like it had broken. She pushed past the ever-growing crowd and ran back, towards the school.

She had left the grounds right away. She had walked right out of the exit, not caring about the shouts of objection coming from the reception staff.

She had run all the way home. Halfway through the journey, the heavens had opened, and she was utterly drenched.

Cars rushed through puddles, splashing her, thoroughly.

At one point a lorry had torn past her at speed, soaking her to the bone.

She could swear, even her underwear was wet through.

She continued to sob as she ran, the rain pelting down, disguising her tears.

She yelled out, periodically in utter shame of what had happened to her.

She could never go back to that school, she thought. She couldn't even think of going on, one more day.

When she got home, she slammed the door behind her.

She chucked her shoes and school bag on the floor where it made a squelching noise as the sodden material hit the hard floor.

She walked into the kitchen sobbing. She began to strip off to her underwear.

She knew that her dad would not be home until late, so she didn't care about walking around, virtually naked.

She shivered from the cold; her damp wet hair stuck to her bare, ghostly white skin.

She placed her clothes in the washing machine, picked up the studded belt from the floor and headed slowly back to the hallway, and up the stairs to her room.

She entered her room, her sanctuary. She looked around at the black walls, covered with posters of bands and legendary skateboarders. She smiled sadly at them, as she slowly lowered herself onto the bed.

She sat that way for a long while, staring at the carpet, unmoving, tears still rolling down her cheeks. She had the absurd thought, 'will I run out of tears?'

With one last burst of energy, she stood quickly and made her way to her dresser. She slipped her underwear off as it was soaked through. Her small breasts prickled at the erected nipple ends, the temperature in the room feeling like icicles, jabbing into her body.

She chose her favourite, comfortable bra and girl boxer shorts.

Following this, she picked up her tartan skirt, ripped at the bottom, to her proud, Scottish fathers' despair.

She popped a halter top on, and then finished the ensemble with her favourite black, velvet jacket, complete with numerous quirky badges.

She sat then in front of the dresser, rearranging her hair, and smiled at herself. She looked OK... apart from her makeup, she thought.

She fixed this too, paying special attention to all the details. She wanted to look as good as she could muster.

When Becca had finished, she sat back and looked at herself, judging her work.

She sighed and smiled sadly. It was how she wanted, she thought to herself.

With that she stood, grabbed the studded belt from the bed and made her way upstairs, to the third floor.

The large space was the converted attic. Her father used it as a den come office.

The old beams of the ancient house were pitted with marks and stained a deep brown, the colour of the darkest chocolate.

She did not delay. She wheeled the office chair over to the closest beam.

With the studded belt in her hand, she gingerly put one foot on the chair and used the back to help steady herself. She lifted the other foot onto the base of the chair.

She stood, balancing carefully, surveying the room.

Oddly, Becca was not scared. She felt at peace. This final

decision warmed her, like a cosy blanket. Soon, the darkness would take her and envelop her like silk. She was almost giddy with anticipation.

Again, she did not hesitate. After the brief survey of the room, she threw one end of the belt over the beam that was just above her head. She then used the other end to place around her long, slender neck and buckled it together, tightly.

She could still breathe easily but the leather cut into her flesh, making the tips of her fingers and toes tingle with the adrenalin that was clearly coursing through her veins.

She began to breathe faster, the breaths becoming shorter. She was afraid the overload of adrenalin would make her pass out, so she proceeded quickly.

With one final, hard tug of the belt (to ensure it was tight and would hold), she stepped swiftly from the chair, ensuring it slid back on its wheels, once her weight was off it.

The belt tightened instantly, squeezing her neck with such veracity, she thought her eyes would pop out. She could sense they were bulging from the restriction, feeling many of the tiny blood capillaries within each eye bursting from the pressure.

Her tongue began to protrude from her mouth which was open wide, subconsciously, gasping for breath. But no air would enter her lungs.

She thrashed around, kicking her legs. It was involuntary, which surprised her. Incoherent thoughts flew through her mind, making no sense, giving no purpose.

A blackness began to enter the very outer edges of her vision.

It grew like a gaping abyss as it enveloped her sight; further and further, till she could see no more.

Her eyes began to dilate; her thrashing slowed to feeble

twitches and her bladder let go; urine spilling down below her onto the carpet.

She made no more sounds as her body, almost imperceptibly swung back and forth.

There was no life left in that body, anymore. The broken shell hung there, awaiting the unimaginable torture of being discovered by Becca's father.

Throughout the whole ordeal, the rain had continued to fall. Mercilessly, it had hammered the skylight windows of the attic room, giving the illusion of a relaxing, white noise, during those final moments of Becca's life.

CHAPTER 31

Jonny watched nonchalantly as Becca headed for the bathroom, then focused on Autumn and smiled.

He caught Becca's almost imperceptible nod in his periphery.

The plan was now active, triggered by Becca's departure.

Jonny's hands had subtly been shaking ever since he had left Becca at the diner's counter. Now that he was again sat in the booth, he tried to breathe slowly and calm his heart, which felt like it was jackhammering in his chest.

Autumn was now fully aware, thanks to Jonny's discreet explanation of the story and their strategy, relayed using coded names and scenarios.

He had successfully kept the conversation encrypted. Autumn was initially at a loss for words as none of it really made any sense.

Before she could ask any questions though, Jonny had persuaded Autumn to collect extra cutlery from the diner's counter. Becca had then subtly intercepted Autumn, swiftly clarifying the real meaning behind Jonny's earlier coded conversation.

Jonny had to give them both credit. Had he not been in on it, he would never have realised they had really spoken, even from his vantage point.

Finally, with Autumn seated once more in front of him, Jonny had gone over parts of the encrypted story and plan, once again.

She had been brilliant, never flinching or raising an eyebrow.

The only time she showed an ounce of emotion, was when

he had explained how Becca had died. He hadn't initially explained this to her, only doing so upon her return from the diner's counter. The subtle emotion from Autumn was the welling of tears in her eyes. He couldn't blame her. The story of Becca's suicide was more than just harrowing. Jonny himself was deeply moved by the story and had to purposely put it to the back of his mind to ensure it didn't affect him at such crucial time.

He was so impressed with Autumn. She truly had the best poker face, he thought. He couldn't help feeling his love for her blossom even more, if that was possible.

His pride for this incredible woman was so palpable, he felt if anything gave them away, it would be that.

Jonny kept his cool as best he could. He ran a hand through his hair and pretended to stretch. As he did so, he looked around to ensure that Ray was still on the far side of the diner, gossiping with another patron. He was. This was ideal, Jonny thought.

It wouldn't be long now, he knew, until he had to stand up to the plate.

His part in this was the lead part, and he had to ensure it went flawlessly. If not, they could all be in for a whole world of hurt.

It felt like the eve of battle. They were going to war after all.

What kept Jonny strong, was not just the love for Autumn nor was it the (hopefully) iron clad plan that himself and Becca had conjured up. What kept him strong and stoic, was that he *knew*, they were doing the right thing. Soon it would all be over, regardless of the outcome.

Just then, Becca came back out of the bathroom and slipped into Wendy's office, unnoticed. Becca closed the door quietly behind her.

That was his cue. He winked at Autumn who in return, gave him a nervous smile and nod. Jonny stood and strode purposefully over to Ray who had begun to head toward the diner's kitchen.

Did he know? Jonny thought. If they were right about Ray, heaven knows what he was capable of and able to unravel.

Jonny hoped this wasn't all for nothing like a big ball of yarn, being shredded by a kitten.

This was no kitten though. This was a vicious cat. A *big* cat that had claws, for sure.

Jonny intercepted Ray smoothly. They met just by the kitchen's door.

'Hey, buddy!' Jonny said, trying to be as light as possible without making it obvious.

He knew he had a good poker face, and he hoped he could keep it up; till it counted at least.

'Jonny! Sorry... I'm quite busy... just need to get Wendy another cup of dirt. I'll chat to you after,' Ray said friendly enough, beginning to push past him for the kitchen door.

Jonny moved sideways to block Ray's path. 'I need to speak to you, Ray,' he said quietly, with a note of conspiracy to his voice.

This seemed to work and get the better of Ray.

'Ohh... dish!' Ray whispered with a smirk, looking around to ensure they weren't being overheard.

Jonny just nodded his head towards the staff room and raised his eyebrows.

Ray seemed to take the hint as he nodded excitedly. Ray headed for the staff room and Jonny followed, closely behind.

Just as they walked through the doorway, he turned back for the briefest of moments to flash Autumn a knowing smile.

She smiled back with the ghost of a wink too.

Ray headed for the couch and sat on the edge of the seat, his back straight, looking expectingly at Jonny.

Jonny took his time. He pulled up a chair, from the corner of the room and sat slowly, across from Ray. The only thing between them was a coffee table. It wasn't going to do much as a barrier to protect him, if it went south, Jonny thought to himself.

Jonny looked into Ray's eyes. Ray raised his eyebrows and said, 'So?'

Jonny smiled at him. It was his time to shine, Jonny thought.

'You're never going to believe this, Ray!' Jonny said, feigning excitement.

Ray grinned at this, clearly enthralled; the anticipation, palpable.

'She *does* want to go... down there!' Jonny began, briefly eyeing the floor. 'She was pretty closed off initially... but I got her to talk. She's a troubled kid after all and it wasn't difficult to get her to open up,' Jonny explained, a sign of arrogance in his voice, that he knew Ray would appreciate.

'Really?' Ray said, drawing the word out. He crossed his legs and lent back, looking at Jonny, thoughtfully.

'Why?' Ray asked, his eyes glowing like fireflies, clearly intrigued.

'Well...' Jonny said, taking his time, drawing everything out and keeping Ray engaged... more importantly... keeping him busy.

'Turns out, she doesn't like it here and is sure she is meant to be... down there!' Jonny continued, a grin on his face.

'I couldn't believe this when she told me... I mean... you always hear that there's somewhere else... for *those* sorts of people.' Jonny said, thoughtfully. He rubbed his beard, and stared at the ceiling, as if in thought.

Jonny waited, purposefully. He wanted Ray to bite. He knew that if he did... he had him; hook, line and sinker.

To Jonny's great relief, Ray did bite.

'Are you saying...' Ray began, trailing off.

Jonny just nodded slowly, his eyes wide.

'Shit!' Ray exclaimed. 'I can't believe it! You're right Jonny... people who take their own lives are meant to go straight down... I've heard, anyway'. Ray said excitedly, adding the last few words quickly, as if an afterthought. 'I mean... its different for them down there... but it's still the rule... as far as I'm aware.' Ray continued, thoughtfully.

Jonny looked at Ray, quizzically, and said, 'It's probably because of her age. Maybe they judge this sort of thing on a case-by-case basis, when it's a kid?' Jonny questioned, leaving it hanging there in the air between them.

Ray looked deep in thought. His brow was furrowed. The hairs on Jonny's neck began to prickle then. A bead of sweat ran down his forehead. He silently prayed in everything that was holy, that Ray was not starting to doubt Jonny.

He didn't know if this was just part of the master manipulation. Did Ray already know about Becca's suicide or was he genuinely unaware? Regardless, Ray had something to gain from this. Whether he knew or not... Jonny knew that Ray was going to try and manipulate him into pushing Becca into leaving.

Ray's features brightened then. He smiled at Jonny and said, 'We need to help her Jonny!'

'Sure... but how, Ray?' Jonny asked.

'Isn't it obvious?' Ray said, raising both his hands in the air as if he was asking God to answer his question, instead of

Jonny.

Jonny looked back at him; confusion plastered across his features.

Ray smiled at him, feigning sympathy as one would to a small child.

He shook his head and said, 'She isn't meant to be here, Jonny... she doesn't *want* to be here either!'

Jonny raised a warning hand and said, 'We don't know that for sure, Ray.'

Ray seemed to think about this comment, briefly. Jonny had always planned to ensure he came across genuine and this included questioning Ray's ideas.

If Jonny didn't know what he knew, he would have dealt with this in the same manner, he thought.

'Come on, Jonny... she told you herself that she's meant to be down there... she wants to go too! Who are we to deny her of that? We need to help her. You've got her ear Jonny... you need to help her.' Ray said, nodding. He was grinning like a Cheshire Cat now too. It made Jonny feel like he wanted to vomit. However, Jonny stoically carried on.

'I dunno Ray... look what happened with Bear and everything...' Jonny mumured, running a hand through his hair, feigning concern. Inside he was elated. He had Ray bang to rights! He knew this was the direction that Ray would lead them. It was all going to plan, he thought.

Jonny silently reminded himself not to get complicit, as the battle was far from over.

'Bear was the Devil, Jonny... the same thing is not going to happen to you!' Ray exclaimed.

'Well, I'm still not sure on that... look at what happened to me in the bathroom last time, remember?' Jonny challenged.

Ray just nodded, pushing his hand through the air as if to

swipe the comment away as unimportant or irrelevant, more likely, Jonny thought.

'Regardless of if he was or wasn't the Devil... you're not Bear, Jonny.' Ray said firmly, still smiling.

Jonny sighed, and said, 'You're right, I'm not Bear. They were pitted against each other you know...' Jonny relayed to Ray. 'Apparently, because they both were "meant" to be down there,' Jonny continued, using air quotes for the word 'meant'.

Ray laughed at this, clearly trying to keep the mood light.

'Well... it looks like old Bear decided to try and send poor Becca down there... either before him...or instead of him!' Ray mused.

Jonny just nodded his agreement. He had had the same thought himself.

'Jonny,' Ray began, his demeanour changing slightly, his features betraying him. It was all business and although a smile still played at his lips, Ray was clearly being deadly serious.

'You've got to help her let go. She trusts you now, clearly. She just needs a hypothetical push is all...' Ray continued, finishing his words with clear anticipation of Jonny's response.

'Maybe you're right, Ray... maybe it's the best thing to do... for her.' Jonny said, looking down, nodding in thought.

He glanced up suddenly and managed to catch the brief glint of a devilish grin on Ray's face. In a microsecond, it was gone though, replaced with an empathetic smile instead.

'God, he is good,' Jonny said to himself. Jonny knew though, that he was arrogant too and full of self-importance.

Just then, before either of them could utter another word, there was a click from the door.

They both turned to look at the closed door. A smile began

to tug at the corners of Jonny's mouth. She had done it, he thought to himself. Becca had convinced Wendy, and now the door was locked.

That wasn't any old lock though, he knew. Jonny's smile turned slowly into a satisfied grin.

Jonny knew (thanks to his earlier cryptic conversation with Autumn, where she had added her own two cents to the plan) that Wendy held a skeleton key. Becca knew this also; again, thanks to Autumn. She had informed Becca when they spoke at the diner's counter.

This key locked and unlocked any door in the diner. Most importantly it was a binding. A binding that sealed against any type of manipulation or force, no matter the strength.

The lights dimmed somewhat suddenly. Jonny had forgotten, momentarily that he was not alone.

He turned back to face Ray, but Ray was gone.

In his place was a terrifying, fetid corpse, going green in some places. It resembled Ray in some way, shape or form... but it was not the Ray that Jonny had come to know, and like, he had to admit.

The cold, dead eyes just stared at Jonny.

Some skin had fallen away from one cheek, revealing the crooked teeth within the thing's mouth. It meant a permanent half smile was constantly grinning at Jonny.

It didn't move, nor did it seem to breathe.

It just sat there. It blinked then and Jonny had to bite his tongue to stop himself from screaming.

Terror was etched on his face; his throat constricted like an albatross around his neck.

The thing that had formally been Ray, was continuing to stare at Jonny, but now it *really* was grinning. The things eyes had changed... they were now completely black. Black as the darkest abyss.

The thing gave Jonny a jaunty wave and then, in a voice that sounded like the literal essence of evil, it said 'Well, well, well.'

CHAPTER 32

Jonny stared at the abomination that sat before him. It continued to grin at him, saying nothing else.

Jonny decided to pluck up the courage and speak. 'You... you can't leave this room!'

It was as much a statement as it was a question. Could this *key* really hold the Devil himself?

The thing in front of him began to laugh then. It nonchalantly inspected it's blackened, elongated nails and spoke, 'You know, Jonny... I may not be able to read minds, but as sure as a bear shits in the woods, I can sure read a poker face... I can smell you too. I can smell the putrid smell of fear... it makes me want to gag, frankly.'

Jonny swallowed hard, not speaking. Sweat dripped from his brow, he wiped it away, absentmindedly.

'Yes, you are correct...' It continued, this time eyeing Jonny with those black, relentless eyes. 'I cannot leave... thanks to you... what I can do though is control you... I'm a master manipulator after all... the original, if you will!' It continued with a chuckle.

'I wouldn't try it.' Jonny said, mustering up his best low voice and menacing stare.

The thing just laughed at Jonny like it was the funniest thing it had ever heard.

It feigned sympathy on it's disgusting features then, and spoke sweetly, 'Aww Jonny. Don't worry!' It sat back with a sigh of content.

'I don't want too!' it continued, happily. 'I don't need to, would be more correct. I was offering you a way out... you and the little bitch in there,' it said pointing to the locked door.

'Why the *fuck* would I ever want to go down there, with you?' Jonny asked incredulously.

The thing feigned pain, it even held it's chest as if Jonny had stabbed it right in its rotten, black heart.

'Jonny! It pains me to hear you speak like that! It really does! Ouch! You seem to think that down there is like the Hell that you've read about in the books and watched at the motion pictures! How wrong you are, tut tut tut,' it mocked. The thing wagged it's greenish, impossibly long finger at him whilst it tutted.

Jonny felt anger rise and blossom like a flower, in his gut. He was so fed up with this crap.

Didn't they say 'rest in peace' for a reason? He just wanted to be left to do just that!

'Bullshit,' Jonny said angrily. 'That place is called Hell for a reason!' he almost shouted.

The thing just laughed at him. 'Calm down, darling! Don't get yourself so worked up. Look, follow my lead... breathe... that's it... in and out... nice and slow...' It said, cackling, unpleasantly.

'Now... don't we feel better?' It asked, mockingly. Clearly not expecting an answer, it continued, 'Look, Jonny... do you know what we call *this* place, down there?'

He simply shook his head at the thing, not caring what it's answer was, yet strangely, he felt he couldn't look away... he could not help but listen. He shook the thought away and focused on the task at hand. 'Keep it busy... it will all be over soon' he said to himself.

The thing didn't seem to notice... or care that Jonny's features had become stone like, obstinance ebbed his features.

'Well... good thing I'm here to tell you then!' it said, smiling, a laugh escaping its dry, blackened lips.

The stench was nearly unbearable for Jonny. He felt like he would throw up at any moment.

'We call this place, "Your Interment." It has a nice ring to it, don't you think?' it said, whilst using air quotes for the words, Your Interment.

Jonny raised an eyebrow at this, but nothing more.

It continued, 'You see Jonny… you are stuck here… pure and simple… you can't go anywhere… apart from this shit hole room!' It raised its hands as if demonstrating the rooms blandness.

'I know that. So, what… it's a holiday down in Hell, is it?' Jonny said sarcastically, a lop-sided grin on his features.

He saw a flash of anger in the thing's eyes, and then it was gone, almost instantly.

'Meow!' it said, laughed. 'It's no picnic, you're right there, old buddy, old pal! But… you do have freedom… bet they don't tell you that in your death meeting, did they?' it purred.

Jonny looked away in disgust. This thing was not going to let up. He just hoped it was all going to plan out in the diner.

Not having a reply, it still continued happily, 'You can move around and go as you please! That's pretty freaking awesome, if you ask me!'

Jonny just shook his head and gave a harsh laugh.

'I don't give a shit what you say… I'd never follow you there… and no one else will either… your time here is up… you're going home… Ray.' Jonny said with more bravado than he thought possible, considering.

It sneered at him then and laughed cruelly.

'Just another day in the office for me, *babe*… and thank you for using my name! Glad you like my *outfit*.'

Jonny stood at this, anger boiling over. His cheeks were

flushed red, and his fists were clenched tight at his sides, the knuckles going white.

'Where is he!' Jonny all but screamed at the thing that sat laughing at him.

'Wow! Sorry, Jonny... little bit of a temper you've got there! Go on... let it all out! I like a guy that's feisty!' it said, jiggling it's hips in the seat, grotesquely.

'Ray was never here, you utter imbecile. It was always me! Ray is back in hell where he belongs. That's what you get for killing your boyfriend. It's easier than you think to get into places that you're not meant to... well... that and I *am* the Devil, after all!' it finished, laughing it's hideous laugh once again.

Jonny felt like the laughter came from all four corners of the room. He held his hands against his ears, trying to drown out the sound. This just made the thing laugh even more. It slapped it's thigh and wiped away tears.

'Enough!' Jonny screamed. It fell silent and sat up straight, eyeing him.

'Handbags! Geez, calm down, Jonny... shall we do another breathing exercise?' it asked, sarcastically.

Jonny smirked then. The Devil did not. It looked angry that Jonny's face now showed resilience rather than anguish.

'You think you're so fucking clever, don't you?' Jonny laughed.

Before the thing could answer, Jonny continued, 'You're just a cunt! Plain and simple. What does it feel like to know that everyone in the universe... alive or dead... thinks you're just an arrogant, good for nothing, twat?' Jonny smirked and gave a harsh laugh.

It was not impressed. It stood and walked slowly, methodically, over to Jonny until they were almost nose to nose.

It's putrid breath made Jonny feel lightheaded, he was certain he would pass out if he was not careful.

Jonny took a single step back. Thankfully, the thing did not move closer.

'You should watch your pretty little mouth, boy... I'm older, wiser and infinitely more powerful than you could ever imagine!' it said in a low rumble.

Jonny could swear the walls actually shook when it spoke. The single strip light above them began to flicker and a breeze had entered the windowless room.

Jonny felt he had reached a fork in the road. One side was to play to the thing's narcissism... the other, to antagonise it more. Jonny went for the latter.

'But you're stuck in a staff room.' Jonny said simply, a condescending look on his features. He even dared to rub his fists below his eyes and said, 'boo hoo!'.

To Jonny's utter surprise, the Devil simply turned, and walked back to the couch where it sat, and crossed its legs. It put its head back and stared at the ceiling.

Jonny watched in silent horror as its scalp flapped back from its forehead, revealing coagulated, blackened blood. It hung there, grotesquely, attached by just a few strands of rotten flesh, before falling off altogether.

Jonny retched at the sight of this and dry heaved a couple of times.

The Devil did not seem to notice, it just let out an exaggerated sigh.

It spoke then, not moving, it just continued to stare at the ceiling. 'I wonder... what would Hattie say, Jonny?' The voice was light and feigned concern and sympathy, all at once.

'I mean... I could ask her when I get home, she is with me

for all eternity, after all,' it continued, this time more cruelly. It couldn't quite hide the malice in its voice.

It lifted its head forward, so that it was facing Jonny. It stared at him with a wide, shit eating grin.

'You're lying.' Jonny said, in a low voice that barely contained his fury.

'You're right. Sorry Jonny. I don't wonder... or frankly give a flying fuck what she thinks... but she is down there... with me... nice and cosy!' it said, smirking, then it leant forward and continued. 'You know... she's a *nasty* girl! She could suck start a leaf blower; I swear! I can't believe you passed that up! Pussy is pussy, after all!' it replied, pure hatred in its ice like words, a nasty chuckle emanating from its dry, wheezing lungs.

It's teeth were gritted now. It was enjoying itself for sure, it was in its element, Jonny thought.

Jonny stared at it stoically. 'I hope your lying. I hope that she is not there... with you. I didn't know Hattie that well. If she is down there... I am truly saddened to hear this. But... you will not torment me by speaking of her. You're a narcissist... and I know narcissists... my ex-girlfriends step mum was the biggest narcissist you'd ever met... in fact she would give *you* a run for your money! My point being... I know what your *kind* are like. If you continue to attempt to torment me... I'll just ignore you. What's worse to a narcissist... than being ignored?' Jonny finished, not expecting an answer. He looked on defiantly, a challenging fire, burning in his wide eyes. He raised his eyebrows, daring the thing to question him.

He then simply walked slowly over to the couch and sat. He picked up a magazine that was dated from five years ago and began to flick through the pages, absentmindedly.

The thing literally hissed with exasperation, from the

other side of the room. It began to move then. It stomped over to the door, the crummy, generic pictures on the walls, shaking with each step.

It banged loudly on the door, making it rattle in its frame. 'Enough! Let me out you peasants!' the thing shouted.

To both Jonny and the things utter surprise, the lock suddenly clicked, and the door swung open. A figure walked through the doorway.

CHAPTER 33

It was Wendy. She strode through the doorway, purposefully. She was followed by Bob, who was close on her heels, like an obedient Labrador.

She smiled kindly at Jonny and then moved her gaze to the thing that stood a few feet from the doorway, pure hatred in its pitch-black eyes.

She stared daggers at the thing, then looked away.

Ignoring it, she walked over to Jonny and hugged him tight. 'You OK, champ?' she asked, kindly, concern in her hazel eyes.

Jonny just stared at her, unblinking. He nodded slowly, not speaking a word.

She smiled back at him reassuringly.

Bob was loitering by the door, clearly uneasy. He moved his weight restlessly from one foot to the other.

They all turned then to look at the thing. It had begun to laugh. It started as a chuckle and ended up being a full throated, belly laugh. It's bone-dry lungs caused a death rattle cough, that ended in a faint wheeze.

It pointed at Jonny shaking it's head, still giggling, but almost silently.

It regained some composure and began to speak. 'This... this is your rescue party?'

Jonny looked around at Bob and then Wendy. He could see the things point.

Jonny cast his eyes down, sadly, feeling despair begin to enter his consciousness.

This just made the thing begin to laugh heartily, once again.

It stopped abruptly then. The thing made its move.

It happened so fast that Jonny could barely see what had happened.

In a flash, the thing had raised its hand. A microsecond later, Bob's long neck was in its grasp, and the thing squeezed, viciously.

Bob yet out a frightened yelp, followed by a whimper. His eyes looked impossibly wide through his thick rimmed glasses.

The overhead strip light seemed to shine brighter then. Jonny noticed it's reflection bounce off of Bob's shiny bald head.

'I'll take that!' The thing said happily and wrenched the key that Bob had been holding, right out of his grasp.

The thing pushed Bob away forcefully. Bob stumbled backwards, nearly falling.

To Jonny, he looked shocked and scared. Bob tried to compose himself but did not speak.

Instead, Wendy did. 'Always with the drama... why did you do that? Now I'm gonna have to take it back off you,' Wendy said, her voice deadly serious.

The thing seemed to consider this for a second... and then burst out laughing. It moved sideways and elbowed Bob in the ribs, shaking it's head in fits of laughter.

It even bent over, placing its hands on its thighs, clearly trying to catch it's disgusting breath.

No one else laughed, although Jonny did look at Wendy, bemused.

How the hell did Wendy think she was going to control this thing, let alone get the skeleton key back off of it? Jonny knew she had balls, but this was suicide! What the hell could she possibly do to it? Jonny continued to muse.

He thought about all the various scenarios that this could end in... none seemed to look like a positive outcome for any of them, except the Devil.

Wendy seemed completely unfazed by the thing's reaction. She turned back to Jonny, ignoring it.

'I'm so sorry, Jonny... I would have been here quicker... but I wasn't in the office, I was out back. Becca found Bob in the office, and he rushed to lock the door,' Wendy explained, nodding at the door with her head, not losing eye contact with Jonny for one moment.

For some strange reason her cool, kind stare, put him at ease.

'He called me as soon as he made it back to the office,' she continued. 'I rushed back as soon as I could. I'm sorry you've had to spend more than a second with this abomination,' she finished, turning to appraise the thing, coolly. She looked away in disgust, almost instantly.

It's laughter had died down, it moved slowly, like a snake towards the couch, where it sat down with a big, theatrical sigh.

Wendy patted Jonny on the shoulder, then said, 'You did good, kid.'

He smiled at her warmly, and she smiled back. She mouthed the words, 'don't worry' to him and he nodded, almost imperceptibly.

The thing (clearly not happy that it was no longer the centre of attention) began to clap, slowly and sarcastically.

'Bravo... bravo, Wendy. I'm impressed... really, I am! You have some serious lady balls... I've got to give you that! Just one question though...' it said, clearly enjoying itself. It feigned thoughtfulness as it spoke, placing a rank finger to its rotten, dry lips and frowned. It scratched its non-existent scalp with the other hand, its elongated, blackened fingers tips coming away covered in thick, congealed blood.

It didn't seem to notice or care, however.

'What... if I may be so brazen to ask... are you... my little dumpling... going to do to stop me?' it continued, as if it was having a happy conversation with a young child.

Jonny knew better though. This was a predator. An evil demon, *the* demon, here only for one purpose. Misery.

Wendy finally turned to face the thing, once again. Her features were tired, and she eyed the thing coolly; a look of almost pity crossing her features.

The look did not go unnoticed. The thing sat up straighter, it's false jovial attitude gone at once. It eyed her, suspiciously, almost cautiously.

Jonny had the distinct feeling that the thing had just picked up on something... perhaps realised something that Jonny did not.

Strangely, he could swear that he noticed the smallest hint of fear creep onto the thing's sagging features.

Whatever it had just worked out... it looked like it was beginning to regret being so narcissistic. If it had paid more attention when Wendy and Bob had first entered the room, perhaps it would have picked up on this... feeling, a lot quicker. Jonny mused over this, thoughtfully.

Wendy approached the thing slowly. There was no malice in her posture or features, yet she walked forward, fearlessly.

The thing noticed this too. Jonny saw for certain now that the thing was on edge, fear glowing in it's dark, evil eyes.

Jonny stole a glance at Bob. He just stood there, expressionless. Jonny could not tell if Bob knew what was going on or not.

As Wendy closed in on the thing, it backed into the corner

of the sofa.

Wendy simply sat next to it, turning so that she faced it, head on.

Alarm was evident in its features now. In a last-ditch attempt to stop whatever it was terrified of (of which Jonny was still none the wiser), it turned back into Ray.

It happened in the blink of an eye. Ray was sat there, looking terrified and helpless.

No sign of the monstrosity that it had been mere moments ago.

'Please... please help me, Wendy... it's got me... it's got me trapped here inside with it!' Ray whimpered.

Wendy did not move a muscle. Her expression did not change. It was still pity that adorned her features, Jonny was sure of it.

Jonny was about to speak out then, as he knew that Ray was not really here.

Wendy spoke before Jonny had a chance though.

'Sorry... but I know where Ray is... he's never been here... you might as well give it up... come on... let's not make this difficult. Leave with your head held high. Do it professionally... don't get upset and let emotion come into play.'

She looked on at the thing, she seemed to be perfectly comfortable and in control of the situation. Her eyes were alive in a way that Jonny had never seen before. Not just from Wendy but from any human he'd ever met.

Instantly, the grotesque thing was back. It snarled angrily at Wendy.

It gritted it's teeth and bit it's lip; blackened blood ran down it's chin and onto its mouldy clothes.

It looked like a caged animal to Jonny, and he was worried that it would turn and bite if Wendy was not careful.

Wendy did not seem to mind though. She looked completely at ease, like a doctor with a patient experiencing a breakdown. She was clearly a professional.

'Touch me and you'll cease to exist,' the thing said to her, its voice barely containing its fury, it's teeth gnashing after it spoke, and foam falling from the corners of its mouth.

Wendy looked away. She focused on nothing in particular. She looked sad then, Jonny thought.

No, not sad, more like disappointed, he realised.

It started as an almost imperceptible soft, white glow. It slowly gained power and became brighter and brighter.

Jonny's eyes were wide in wonder as he watched. This white, mythical glow was emanating from Wendy herself.

As it grew brighter still, Jonny had to squint and shield his eyes.

It then became unbearable. Jonny had to look away. He squeezed his eyes tightly shut.

A noise had begun now too. It was a soft humming sound. It was quite pleasant, Jonny thought.

Then he heard the inhuman, demonic scream come from the couch.

Jonny knew right away that it was the Devil, and it was in pure agony.

CHAPTER 34

The dazzling, other worldly light and hypnotic humming sound began to wane.

Jonny's eyes were still tightly squeezed shut. He raised his hands to cover his eyes, and slowly opened them.

Gingerly, he parted his fingers to survey the room.

The light and sound had now almost completely disappeared.

Apart from Jonny, the room was now empty.

There was a slight mist or fog, lingering in the room at knee level. The door that led back into the diner was open wide.

Jonny slowly made his way to the doorway.

Cautiously, he peaked round the door frame and inspected the space beyond. All was quiet and gloomy in the antechamber. The other doors that lead to the kitchen and storeroom, were closed.

Jonny warily stepped through the staff room's doorway. He made his way out of the antechamber and into the diner.

As he entered the diner, everything seemed to be in slow motion.

Every single person in the diner was shielding their eyes; some were cowering in their seats. Everyone except Wendy. She stood near the entrance, her legs wide, in a fighting stance. Her left hand was up, palm facing towards the door. The same brilliant white light that seemed to shroud her, was pulsating from her palm.

Jonny was surprised that the holy looking glow around her no longer affected him. He assumed it was because her back was fully turned to him. It also seemed to Jonny, that the potency or strength of the light was being focused on what was erupting out of her palm.

Jonny watched in shocked awe, as the door opened and the black abyss, which was once Ray, began to move through it. The thing no longer had any discernible shape. It was just a large, dark mass. It was still terrifying to look at, and Jonny periodically looked away, scared to stare at it too long.

It was almost graceful, the way the hideous dark mass almost floated through the doorway and out into the gloom of the night.

Thunder and lightning crashed so loudly, it felt like it was inside the diner itself.

The entire building shook to its foundations. Dust and other particles littered the floor, falling from all around the diner.

A deep, thick fog began to creep in from outside, encasing the black mass like a tomb.

The thing was nearly completely outside now.

The weather seemed to be at a crescendo. The light from Wendy's palm growing brighter still.

Wind swept through the large room. Menus and other papers whipped around like they were in a vortex.

Wendy's short hair was being blown in all directions, the vortex seemed to be focused on what was most powerful at the core, which was of course, Wendy.

In a sudden, somewhat anti-climactic end, it was suddenly all over.

The black mass disappeared in the blink of an eye. The door slammed shut and with it, the wind, fog and worsened weather, left instantly.

Jonny looked around in amazement, noticing the dazzling light had now gone from Wendy's palm. She was slowly putting her hand back down, to rest at her side.

There was still a warm glow, radiating from her body, but that too, was dwindling.

The lights, which had been periodically flickering, now shone steadily.

The other people in the diner began to rectify themselves, brushing the debris from their clothes and straightening knocked over glasses and salt and pepper shakers.

They all looked around in bewilderment. The haunting looks on their faces was the same as what Jonny imagined his own face looked like.

They all seemed to be silently questioning, 'is it over?'.

Wendy had turned then and smiled around the room, warmly.

Bob, who had been sheltering in a nearby booth, stood, straightened his clothes and moved to be by Wendy's side, once again. Her loyal, right-hand man.

Wendy said nothing. She began to walk down the centre aisle and headed for the office.

As she approached Jonny, she turned to him and said, 'Please follow us, Jonny.'

He obliged, unquestioningly.

The three of them entered the office. Bob began to close the door when a well-manicured, delicate hand appeared, stopping it from closing all the way.

The door was forced back open. Autumn stood there; concern etched across her features.

Bob spoke up and said in an apologetic voice, 'Sorry, Autumn. Wendy needs to speak to Jonny before she speaks to the rest of the diner.'

Autumn looked at him, then at Wendy with a defiant look in her eyes. She held her head high and spoke. 'I am with

Jonny. Whatever you say to him, you say to me,' she said simply but firmly.

Bob looked confused, he turned to face Wendy who just smiled and nodded once.

Bob gave Autumn a look that seemed to say, 'OK then' and she entered, closing the door behind her.

Jonny sat in the same seat he had occupied earlier. Wendy did not sit down, however. Instead, Bob wheeled the chair round for Autumn to sit in, next to Jonny.

Autumn thanked Bob and sat, looking around the room, her features deep with concern.

Wendy stood behind the desk, looking around the room, a smile still on her lips.

Bob came over and stood beside her, once again.

'What the hell is going on, Wendy?' Autumn blurted out, her eyes were wide and afraid.

Wendy simply raised her hands as if to calm her. 'Do not worry. I will explain,' Wendy said. Her voice was calm, and it seemed lower to Jonny. It was different too, in a way that Jonny could not workout or understand.

Wendy smiled at them both warmly and then spoke again, softly. 'Thank you, Jonny. Thank you both. You have done us a great service by working out that Ray was not who we all thought he was.'

Jonny didn't know what to say to this, so he simply nodded and smiled.

Wendy seemed to think for a moment, before speaking again. 'I've personally known for some time that the gatekeeper was here amongst us. I did not say anything, as even I was not sure who it was.'

She smiled then, which turned into a small grin. 'I had my suspicions... but when Bear left, it made everything more difficult. I knew the essence of evil was still amongst us... yet I still was not certain... who it actually was,' she continued, thoughtfully.

Jonny stole a glance at Autumn. She was sat on the edge of her seat, her lips slightly parted, her eyes wide. She looked completely awestruck by the conversation, mesmerised even.

Jonny returned his focus to Wendy.

'The gatekeeper is an arrogant, evil thing. How you and your friends deduced that something was not right with Ray, and subsequently managed to corner him and get him to speak the truth, is nothing less than miraculous,' Wendy said, smiling, a soft twinkle in her deep, hazel eyes.

Jonny felt almost tongue tied at that moment. He didn't know how to respond.

'Thank you... it was all Jonny's plan... thankfully it worked as we hoped,' Autumn said, speaking up, clearly noticing Jonny was struggling for words.

Autumn smiled at Jonny proudly; he returned the smile and touched her arm in a silent thanks.

'As Jonny will undoubtedly explain to you, Autumn,' Wendy began. 'Ray was never here... it was purely a disguise for the gatekeeper. The real Ray... although I'm sure very similar to the Ray you thought you knew... is down there, where he is meant to be,' she continued, briefly eyeing the floor.

Jonny, Autumn and Bob, looked down at the glass floor, all at the same time. Thankfully, his chair was still on the big rug, Jonny thought.

'Now I must confess something myself,' Wendy said, this time with a little regret in her voice.

'I'm sorry that you had to find out this way. It was necessary though I assure you. I had to be here... to know for sure... that the gatekeeper was indeed here. I knew as soon as I entered. I had to stay though... I had to ensure I was here when the gatekeeper inevitably made his presence known... or when he was discovered,' she continued.

The last words were spoken lighter, a knowing grin playing at her lips as she eyed Jonny.

Both Jonny and Autumn stared at Wendy, complete confusion clear on their features.

Wendy smiled at them patiently, but it was Bob who spoke up.

'Sorry... just wanted to say... it might make it a bit easier to understand...' Bob eyed Wendy carefully to ensure he was allowed to continue to speak, it seemed to Jonny.

She simply smiled at him, and he continued. 'Yeah... so... Wendy is or has... actually retired now... she left a while ago... before you got here, Jonny.'

Stupidity was not one of Jonny's weaknesses, he felt. He knew there was something major going on; he had noticed this in the staff room. However, he still couldn't work out the complete story.

This comment from Bob, just made understanding the situation even more perplexing.

Wendy laughed softly then. The sound was like nature itself, gently flowing between the dark, green leaves of a forest.

'I think...' she began. 'That that may have confused the poor loves even more, I'm afraid Bob!' she continued, smiling.

Bob smiled, sheepishly and looked away.

Wendy focused on them both then. 'He is right though, about Wendy. As I am sure you can guess, that means I'm not Wendy. I am from... up there,' she said, slowly pointing upwards.

They all looked up briefly and then Jonny focused his gaze back on Wendy, wonder in his eyes.

Wendy smiled at Jonny and spoke again, in the same soft voice. 'I... am the gatekeeper of Paradise'.

CHAPTER 35

The first emotion that passed through Jonny was not amazement nor was it wonder or even relief. To his surprise, he felt anger, starting in his chest and slowly rising to his head.

Jonny felt deceived. He had spent a long time with this person, discussed and shared exceptionally private stories. He felt duped. His face clearly showed this.

'Please do not feel that I lied to you, Jonny... especially not on purpose,' Wendy spoke.

Before Jonny could reply, she continued, 'Wendy may not have been here since you arrived... but I have spoken on her behalf.'

Both Jonny and Autumn looked at her incredulously.

She smiled at them both and raised her hands as if surrendering.

'I know... it's easy to say it... but let me ask you this, Autumn...' she began, focusing her attention on Autumn.

'Everything I've said to you... and that Jonny has relayed to you since he's been here... does that match with what Wendy has said or done previously?' she continued, somewhat cryptically.

Jonny looked from Wendy to Autumn. She seemed to be in thought... almost weighing up the response that she would give.

Autumn chose to simply nod in response. Wendy took this as a sign to continue.

'I have the ability to not just look like someone else but to also obtain their personality.

I did this with Wendy... obviously with her full consent.

As she had previously worked here and had not confirmed her retirement date with you all, it seemed an ideal cover for my visit,' she said and then turned slightly to focus on Bob.

'Bob was the only one who knew... that is, he knew who I *really* was and my objective... to find the Gatekeeper for below.' She finished, placing her hands on top of one another, smiling at Jonny and Autumn.

'So, in a sense... you were Wendy?' Jonny asked, confusion in his voice.

'That's correct, Jonny,' she replied simply.

'What's your real name?' Autumn asked.

'I think it would be best to continue calling me Wendy... that, or Gatekeeper,' she replied kindly.

'Gatekeeper.' Jonny repeated to himself. His brow was furrowed as he continued to process the recent revelation.

'So, if the Gatekeeper of... down there... is the Devil... then that means you're...' Jonny began but trailed off before he could finish his sentence.

Wendy... or more correctly... the Gatekeeper looked on knowingly, a sparkle in her eyes. She did not answer. Just then, Bob jumped in.

'Uh... guys... sorry but we have quite a bit to deal with here... immediately though, we need to discuss something important with you, Jonny...' he said, again in an apologetic voice.

Jonny decided to let the clear diversion and change in subject go. He had to admit, he was curious to find out what they wished to discuss with him. After all, it was done now, complete. What else could there be to sort out, he wondered to himself.

Autumn looked at Bob, then to Wendy, confusion ebbed across her soft features.

She bit her bottom lip and said, 'Can I stay for this? Please.'

'Of course,' Wendy said kindly.

Wendy then turned to focus her full attention on Jonny. It was odd to Jonny; it was not just that she solely looked at him... but also, he could physically feel in his bones that she was now focused just on him, and him alone. It was as if he was the only person in the universe. It felt amazing, he had to admit.

Before she could speak, Jonny decided to squeeze one last question in. 'Don't you need to be anywhere else right now?' He said quickly, a knowing smile on his lips.

'Is that a test, Jonny?' Wendy replied with a smirk. Before he could respond, she once again spoke. 'I know you've already asked that about the Gatekeeper for below... you're not stupid so you know the answer will be the same for me...'

Jonny smiled at her; his cheeks flushed with embarrassment and something else... was it shame? He couldn't explain it, but he felt like he must show himself in the best possible light in front of this... being. He really didn't want to come across as anything but the very best version of himself.

'Sorry,' he all but whispered.

She smiled at him warmly and gave a small chuckle. To Jonny, there was no other word for how it sounded... heavenly.

'It's fine, Jonny. To confirm... I can be in countless places at once... so do not worry... nothing will go amiss whilst I am here with you both.' She said in a warm, happy voice.

Both Jonny and Autumn smiled at her in response.

Jonny felt butterflies in his stomach then. He didn't know what they were about to discuss, but he felt that somehow it was important. He just knew that this was a pivotal point in his life... or afterlife.

'Jonny,' Wendy said simply. 'You have done this place a huge service. In the face of pure evil and danger… you came through and did something truly courageous, selfless, and pure,' Wendy said formally, pausing to briefly look at Bob and then returning her attention to Jonny. She smiled at him reassuringly.

'A Gatekeeper has never been needed for Purgatory. There are many reasons for this. Thanks to your actions, however, I will now be ensuring that I split my time between both here… and up there,' she continued, briefly pointing upwards.

Jonny simply smiled at Wendy, a slight flush in his cheeks was still evident.

'You remember what I said regarding leaving this place early, yes?' she queried.

Jonny simply nodded. Just then, Bob lent over the desk and placed a file in front of Wendy. Jonny took a sharp intake of breath as he noticed, albeit upside down, that his name was printed on the top of the file. This was the same file that he had seen on his first visit to Wendy's office. Bob opened it to a page at the very back.

The page was a different colour to the rest. It was bright orange. Wendy briefly scanned down it and then looked up again at Jonny, smiling.

'Jonny. Due to your heroism, you are now being offered your chance to leave Purgatory,' she said to him; her voice was again very formal, yet her eyes still twinkled.

Jonny's mouth fell open. He looked from Wendy to Autumn. She equally seemed to be in shock.

Jonny focused back on Wendy as she once again began to speak.

'You have the three options to consider, Jonny. Firstly, to stay here and continue your time, until it is complete.

Secondly, to be reborn... but please remember the caveats that I explained, regarding this.

Last but not least... you have the choice... to ascend... yet you will have to return periodically to Purgatory to work. This will continue until your time is served, of course.'

Jonny had to catch his breath. He was in utter shock. How could this be? He had been here such a short amount of time... but he was already being offered the chance to leave!

'Are you sure?' he blurted out.

Wendy gave a short but kind laugh. 'Of course!' she said simply, smiling kindly.

Bob then jumped in again. 'I'm sorry, Jonny... but we will need you to make a decision... pretty much immediately on this... sorry, it's just the way it works,' he said in sombre voice.

Jonny looked at Autumn then. She was staring at nothing in particular. She seemed numb. A tear ran down her cheek. She wiped it away and finally turned to look at him.

She smiled sadly and spoke. 'I've only just got you back, Jonny... but you have to take this chance and go!' Her voice was fragile but firm.

Jonny shook his head vehemently.

'I'm not leaving you, Autumn. I love you and I'd rather be with you, here... than up there without you!' he said forcefully.

She shook her head slowly at him. 'No, Jonny. You must go. I will join you again one day... you know that,' she said, sadness lacing her words.

Jonny turned to Wendy then. A pleading look in his eyes. 'Wendy... come on... Autumn can come too... and Becca... they both helped me... significantly, in fact!' He said, almost begging.

Wendy smiled at him sadly. 'It's just you, Jonny. Everyone's situation is different. This is for you, and you alone.' She said softly but firmly.

Jonny shook his head once again, staring down at the floor, exasperated.

Bob spoke up then, tentatively. 'You know Jonny... everyone's Paradise... is their own. You could be there with Autumn... even when she is down here... it's your choice... you can have whatever your heart desires. When she ascends... you can truly join paradises if you wish... or even have one you share and one for yourself, just for you.'

Jonny could tell Bob was trying to help but all it did was frustrate Jonny. He could feel himself getting angry like a child who couldn't work out a new game right away.

He stared daggers at Bob. 'I do not want a *fake* Autumn, thank you, Bob,' he spat.

Jonny began to cry then. He was exhausted and this was a step too far for him. The tears fell freely. The dam he had held up for so long broke.

It really was the true essence of Purgatory. Everything you want except the thing you want the most. It was so messed up, he thought bitterly.

Autumn spoke again then. 'Jonny... babe... you have to take this opportunity. I will find you when I ascend. We will be together again... for all eternity. If not for you then do it for me... please!' Her voice almost broke him. She was begging him to leave her, yet he knew she loved him as much as he loved her. It was such a cruel scenario to find himself in.

Wendy looked at them both with genuine sadness. 'I'm sorry this is such a hard decision. Please think carefully about your choice,' she said softly, looking over to Bob who nodded slowly in agreement.

Tears rolled down Jonny's cheeks. He stared at his hands,

clenching his fists in frustration.

He looked over at Autumn. She smiled at him sadly, clearly trying to be strong for him. Her eyes were truly dazzling. They seemed to be conveying to him, that everything would be OK. He smiled at her then and turned to Wendy.

'Wendy... there is no other choice, right?' he asked quietly.

'I'm afraid not, Jonny.' Wendy answered, softly.

Jonny sighed deeply and glanced once more at Autumn before speaking.

'OK, Wendy. I choose Paradise.'

CHAPTER 36

The short time after the meeting, felt shorter still. That is to say, Jonny felt it passed within the blink of an eye.

In what felt like a matter of hours, the time had come for him to leave.

He had said his goodbyes to the patrons of the diner, including some one-on-one time with a few, such as Becca.

Becca had been gracious and understanding with the news that Jonny would be leaving. She admitted to Jonny that she would have done the same in his situation.

Becca also informed him that leaving, for someone such as herself, was a little more complex. Due to the sad nature of her death (being that it was self-inflicted), it was more complicated. She did not reveal any more information to Jonny, and he did not wish to pry. He assumed it was private. At any rate, he would soon learn about all the small print when he became a cog in the machine that was the institution.

Purgatory was like a business in that sense. It needed customers and it needed staff. Jonny was simply leaving as a customer and returning as an employee.

He had confided in Becca that he was incredibly nervous. It wasn't just the fact that he was leaving and in turn, leaving Autumn, but also that he was entering uncharted territory.

There was no rule book or instruction manual to read and follow to prepare you for your 'forever' afterlife.

Paradise, he was sure, would be exactly that, Paradise! Yet he was terrified all the same.

Jonny had dealt with change well in life. That is not to say he enjoyed it though. Like many, he loathed change. He would often take a different path, if it meant not having to make hard decisions that would inevitably end up in change. Even if this held him back or created a complicated situation for him, he would often prefer this to the alternative.

After his conversation with Becca, Jonny had made a point of visiting Wendy once more.

Bob had left by then. He had simply wanted to thank her, which he did.

It was a brief meeting, but one that he felt was worth having. Wendy had given a speech to the diner after the meeting with himself, Autumn and Bob.

She had explained that the Devil, had in fact been Ray.

Everyone had been flabbergasted, understandably. She had soothed them, answered several questions and then left in an elegant fashion.

She had not explained to them her true identity. For that, Jonny was thankful. He knew how much it would be for everyone to take in.

He had to admit though; it wasn't the only reason. He had a certain feeling of pride, knowing that he was in on the secret. Jonny was no show-off and certainly not one for being overconfident. However, the feeling that he knew a little more than most of the others gave him a superior feeling, he had to admit rather embarrassingly. He felt this was somewhat arrogant and therefore, did not share it with Becca or Autumn – but he knew it was there, which created guilt, deep within him.

He was only human after all... or had been. He had relayed this only to Wendy, in not so many words.

She had just smiled knowingly at him. She had said he should not feel guilty. Wendy had also thanked him for saying nothing to anyone.

She felt it was better this way. Those who didn't know,

could be blissfully unaware and untroubled. Jonny agreed wholeheartedly.

Before the end of the one on one with Wendy, he had explained that his last (and most important) farewell, to still be had, was with Autumn.

They had of course spoken already, but this was to be their private farewell, in the staff room.

It was something that Jonny dreaded. He knew what was coming. They were going to say goodbye.

Neither knew how long for, which just made it harder.

They had agreed together that they should say their goodbyes privately. After this, Jonny would leave and that would be that.

One day, hopefully soon, they would again be reunited and that is what would give them both hope.

All of this and more passed quickly through Jonny's mind as he walked slowly towards the back of the diner, heading for the staff room.

As he passed various booths, people offered their congratulations, some thanked him for alerting Wendy to Ray's true identity. Others simply smiled or nodded their heads in acknowledgment.

It meant a lot to Jonny. Every person who he made eye contact with gave him a positive reaction. This in turn gave him more strength during every step, to complete his journey.

He glanced over to Becca as he finally approached the kitchen's antechamber. She had simply smirked, winked and given him the universal rock and roll sign with her hand. He had returned the gesture and had smiled widely at her.

Before he knew it, the door to the staff room was closing, silently behind him.

He looked around the shabby room, taking it all in, one

last time.

Jonny then focused on the slender figure of Autumn, sat alone on the sofa.

She looked so delicate. Jonny had the crazy notion that if he touched her, she would turn to ash before him.

He approached her gingerly. She looked up, her big green eyes focusing on him. She smiled warmly, yet her eyes conveyed sadness and worry.

Jonny stopped before her, a look of complete surprise on his face.

Autumn looked at him, confused.

'What is it, Jonny?' she asked, concern thick in her voice.

He smiled widely then and laughed.

'I just realised... I cannot believe that I never commented on that beautiful dress that you're wearing!' he said, delight in his voice.

She giggled and smiled back at him. 'I didn't want to say anything, but I was surprised you hadn't asked about it. Don't forget it was what I was wearing the last time I saw you.' she said, jovially.

Jonny smirked, and in a deep, faux seductive voice he murmured, 'You weren't wearing anything the last time I saw you on earth, babe.'

Autumn laughed out loud at this, placing well-manicured fingers across her mouth.

As her laughter subsided, she said, 'that is true!'

'Seriously though, how did I not bring this up earlier?' Jonny said, his voice higher than usual.

'I don't know, babe. You've had a lot going on since you've been here... it hasn't stopped... perhaps that's why.' She said thoughtfully.

'True... but still. To be honest, Autumn... I think seeing

you again is what did it. I see through it all... I see you. That is what has truly amazed me. Seeing the dress now and focusing on its glory... it's just an addition... an accompaniment that accentuates your beauty.' Jonny said, smiling kindly.

'Big words Mr. However, that won't help you get in my pants!' Autumn said, laughing.

'Sorry... that was really cringey, I just realised!' Jonny replied, also laughing.

'Cringey, but lovely. Thank you, Jonny.' Autumn replied, a little more seriously.

He nodded in response and smiled happily, although sadness began to envelop his heart.

Autumn noticed and said, 'What's wrong?'

Jonny swallowed the lump in his throat and said quietly, 'I don't want to leave you, babe.'

Autumn smiled at him sadly. She beckoned him over and he obliged.

He sat down next to her, and they embraced. They hung on to each other, as if for dear life.

Both wept openly.

'We will get through this, Jonny. You hear me?' she whispered into his ear. The defiance in her voice was palpable.

He nodded; his face pressed into her sweet-smelling hair. He held her tighter still.

Autumn lifted her head then and stared into his eyes, stroking his face.

'I don't want our last memories of this place to be sad, Jonny,' she said simply.

She stood then, holding his hand. She led him over to the other side of the room.

There, a blanket was laid out on the floor with several cushions from the sofa, creating an inviting bed.

Jonny smiled at Autumn. She smiled back. No words passed between them, but they silently agreed that this was how they wanted to spend their last moments together in Purgatory.

Slowly, they both began to undress. When they got to their underwear, they lay down, embracing each other, once again.

Autumn's large breasts pressed against Jonny's chest warmly. She giggled as the coarse chest hair tickled her erect nipples. He laughed in response and stroked her long, dark hair.

Not for the first time, Jonny was glad for several reasons that she wore no bra. The magnificent gown that now lay next to them on the floor, did not seem to require one.

Autumn kissed him then, soft and long. He felt himself begin to grow hard. She clearly noticed also as he could feel her grin within their kiss.

Whilst not losing contact for one second, she expertly slid her dainty thong down her thighs, and to her feet. Using her toes, Autumn cleverly gripped the garment and slipped it off her feet altogether.

Jonny was impressed. He certainly could not do the same; not in such an elegant fashion anyway. He had to begrudgingly break away from their embrace to slide down his boxers.

His engorged penis stood proudly erect between them both.

'Seven inches… on a good day,' Autumn teased, reminiscing for a moment on past memories where they had laid together, talking and laughing after love making.

Jonny laughed at this, the memories rushing back to him also.

After this, they did not speak again.

They kissed slowly and passionately.

She groped for his erect penis and wrapped her small, delicate hand around it. The well-manicured nails lightly biting into the skin, making Jonny gasp with pleasure.

He felt her smile once again through their kiss.

Jonny returned the favour and slid his hand between Autumns thighs. She lifted one leg, just slightly, so that he could touch and tease her, in the most sensitive of areas.

She too gasped in pleasure as he touched her soft, delicate skin. He rubbed the slick area tentatively, the touch well versed.

Jonny was surprised at how aroused Autumn already was... that being said, he could not speak, he felt himself ready to burst both physically and mentally.

In a swift movement, Autumn rolled him to his back and in no time at all was atop him.

With practiced ease, she allowed him to enter her. Hot, warm flesh enveloped his rock-hard member. Jonny and Autumn, both sighed in utter ecstasy.

She sat up straight, her body an elegant masterpiece in Jonny's eyes. It was as if her delicate curves were sculptured by the gods themselves, he thought in wonder.

Autumn moved slowly and rhythmically up and down. Jonny watched in childlike amazement as her taught body moved with the grace of an otherworldly being.

Her large breasts heaved as she breathed deep, her eyes tightly closed in concentration and utter bliss.

Autumn began to move faster, with more urgency. Her breasts shaking with each impact, every time she came to briefly rest on his pelvis. This became more forceful, making him close his eyes also, the pleasure was almost too much to endure.

He could sense that climax was not far away for either of

them. He raised his hips to meet her, giving Autumn every inch of himself both physically and emotionally.

Jonny realised then that this was true love making at its essence.

The saying gets thrown around so much, but he knew then, that 'making love' to someone truly had meaning. It meant maintaining and growing one's love for one another, through this, the most private and sensational physical acts.

It truly did complete their love, he thought to himself as he felt the imminent eruption began to build pressure and force its way to the surface.

Their love making was not lustful, it was intimate and incredibly special to them both. Neither wanted it to finish, but as with all good things, they must come to an end.

The climax came for both of them, simultaneously. It truly was breath taking in every sense of the word. They both yelling out their sensual gratifications.

She slid from him and lay breathlessly at his side, draping a hand across his somewhat barrel-like chest.

They still did not speak. They just shared in each other's glory; awe inspired by the earth-shattering moment they had just shared. It had always been amazing, but this truly was from another realm. A mythical, heavenly place, that neither wanted to ever leave.

They held each other tight, the sweet smell of Autumn's perfume intoxicating Jonny.

Within moments, it seemed, both fell into a deep, dreamless and satisfying sleep.

A quiet but persistent knocking roused Jonny from his slumber.

He crept silently from the makeshift bed, slipping on his clothes as quickly as he could.

He opened the door slowly, just a crack. Wendy smiled at him through the gap. She did not speak, but he knew why she was there.

He whispered, 'Is it time?' she simply nodded in answer to his question.

Jonny sighed deeply and nodded sadly. He suddenly had a thought, opening the door a little wider.

'Wendy. Do you have a pen I can borrow?' he asked.

She patted herself down and brought a pen out of a pocket. She handed it to Jonny with a smile and said, 'I'll be in my office.'

He smiled in response and quietly closed the door.

Jonny went and sat on the couch, gently. He carefully removed his wallet from a pocket, trying to make as little noise as possible. He pulled out the old, folded note from Autumn.

He turned it over to the blank side and wrote a quick message. He then got up, placed the note on the pillows beside Autumn's sleeping head, and left.

Jonny closed the door behind him as he entered the office. Wendy stood at the back of the room, next to the mysterious door that somehow led to the corridor, where Bob had entered, previously.

Jonny began to walk over to her slowly, but she raised her hand to stop him.

'Before you go, Jonny. I need you to sign the document in your file.' she said and pointed to her desk.

He smiled, grabbed the pen that he had borrowed from Wendy, showing her. She smiled her encouragement as he walked over to the desk.

He looked down at the orange document. Jonny noticed a big red tick by the third paragraph. This seemed to detail his choice to leave for Paradise but return periodically to work.

He signed his name at the bottom where it indicated to do so. He placed the pen on the folder and looked up, expectantly.

Wendy raised her eyebrows and held out a hand towards the door, saying nothing.

Jonny approached her apprehensively.

She smiled at him warmly. 'Do not worry, Jonny,' was all that she said.

'How do I know when to or... where to go for work, Wendy?' Jonny asked, knowing he was stalling somewhat.

She smiled again at him and placed a hand softly on his shoulder.

'Don't worry about that, Jonny. You will find out all those details when you've settled in. Please just enjoy your afterlife, you deserve it after all. Thank you again,' she said.

Her brow furrowed slightly then, and Jonny looked at her quizzically.

'Sorry... I just have to ask Jonny, why the note?' she queried.

Jonny smiled, he had anticipated this question, full well knowing that Wendy must have known what he was doing.

'I couldn't say goodbye, Wend. As we have a history with notes... I thought it was a truly romantic gesture. I hope she sees it that way anyway,' Jonny mused to himself, more than to Wendy.

Wendy smiled and said, 'I'm sure she will, Jonny.'

'I couldn't say goodbye as I'll never say it again. That I pledge to you. I love you. I cannot wait to be beside you once again,' Jonny relayed the note out loud from memory. It was at the forefront of his mind after all.

'Beautiful,' Wendy said simply, smiling at him. She then

ushered him with her hand towards the door.

Jonny nervously nodded his understanding and walked up to it. He smiled at Wendy once more, which she returned.

He then placed his hand on the cool surface of the door's handle.

He pushed the lever down easily and pulled. The door begrudgingly began to move, and Jonny had to put some force into the action.

Finally, the door gave way, and he swung it wide open.

A dazzling, bright white light enveloped his entire being.

He did not hesitate, nor did he look at Wendy again. He knew if he did, he may never leave.

Jonny purposefully strolled into the magnificent, blinding light; the door slowly closing behind him with an audible click.

EPILOGUE

The deep, haunting bass reverberated through the thick, sound-proofed wall. Small particles of dust were released from various trinkets that adorned the walls shelves.

The effect was not particularly intrusive. Yet after some time, it did become somewhat exasperating. The suited individual walked quickly past the double doors where the sound was most prominent.

Juggling the big gulp and a small box of popcorn, the individual finally made it to the back office. It was labelled Manager.

In no time at all, the individual was hunched over the large, cluttered desk in the fishbowl-like office.

The shift had only begun recently, and the manager's suit jacket had already been tossed carelessly onto the chair opposite the desk.

His tie was pulled loose around his neck, and his shirt was untucked at the back.

The name badge that adorned the already creased white shirt, was askew.

The badge declared that its owner's name was Jonny.

Irritation was abundant on Jonny's handsome, rugged features. His brow was deeply furrowed as he concentrated on the file that lay open in front of him.

A small but still significant pile of almost identical files sat to the right of the desk.

Jonny eyed them and hissed through his teeth in exasperation.

His second shift. That was all it was, and he already had a pile of work to catch up on.

How was that fair? His first shift had been a crash course in understanding what his job was. Following that, it had been learning what went on behind the scenes.

Jonny sat back in his chair, which groaned loudly. He knew he was procrastinating, yet he couldn't help thinking about everything. What his brain had endured, the last time he was here, was bordering on torture. His mind asked the question again, 'how is this fair?'

Jonny stood, stretching his back and letting out a long, loud sigh. At least the office was silent, he thought to himself. Even if it was a fishbowl with its glass walls, floor and ceiling.

Jonny briefly waved at the woman sat behind the desk in the adjoining office.

She gave a tired smile and continued devouring the file that lay in front of her.

There was a knock at the manager's door then.

Jonny rolled his eyes and walked over, opening it.

He inwardly sighed as he instantly recognised the short, young raven-haired woman that stood in the doorway.

She smiled at him and pushed past his large frame, without being invited in. Jonny turned and followed her, a slouch in his posture.

He sat in his chair, opposite the girl who had already seated herself. She clearly hadn't noticed, or more likely, didn't care that his jacket was now crushed under her weight.

Her large dark eyes blinked and looked around the office with an air of arrogance.

The girl irritated Jonny, but he could not help staring at her. He always did when he had to deal with her questions or complaints.

She wore an insanely revealing nurses' outfit, splattered with (what he hoped was) fake blood. The one-piece outfit was so short that he could see the tops of her white stockings. The tantalising flash of black underwear caught Jonny's eye also, as she crossed her legs.

He chided himself for the involuntary gasp; he hoped she hadn't noticed.

The already revealing top half of the nurse's dress was exaggerated further by a deep tear. It began at her ridiculously large cleavage and went off to one side, revealing pale, blemish free skin beneath.

He glanced briefly at the girl's bosom, which was practically bursting out of the scanty outfit.

Jonny raised his eyes quickly, noticing the smirk on the heavily made-up face of the girl. A slow, seductive smile parted her deep red lips, revealing perfect white teeth. She clearly knew what her appearance did to any red-blooded man.

'They're the real thing, you know,' she said in an overly husky voice, a lop-sided grin adorning her pretty mouth.

Jonny ignored the comment, trying to focus. He spoke quickly, 'What can I help you with, Amy?'

Her demeanour changed then. It was all business.

'Raising the Titanic... again, really?' was all she said, irritation lacing her voice.

Before Jonny could reply, she continued to rant. 'I mean, the first time... I was like...this sucks...and it's old, not to mention completely wrong! The ship broke in half for God's sake!' She brushed a loose raven lock from her pretty face, rolling her eyes.

If she didn't have such a vile personality, she would be a complete ten, Jonny thought to himself, amused.

Once again, Jonny didn't have a chance to answer.

'After like ten times, I've had enough, Jonny. We watch

that damn film every week, I swear. You must change it!' she continued, in a demanding tone.

Jonny sighed and leant back in his chair, eyeing the office above him.

'You know the score, Amy,' he said tiredly, still looking up. 'This is what Purgatory is. It's the middle of the road, hence the films are acceptable... at best.'

He leant forward then, meeting her eyes.

She frowned at him, clearly not pleased with the answer.

'Besides,' Jonny continued, 'I don't decide what you watch, I've told you this numerous times. I will, however, pass on your concerns, once again,' he finished.

She stood quickly, crossing her arms over her bulging chest. She let out a loud sigh. Jonny wouldn't have been surprised if she stamped her feet like a petulant child.

'This is shit, Jonny. Why am I stuck in a frigging cinema? I'm not even a huge movie buff!' she all but shouted.

'Also, as I've explained to you before, Amy... the system is fool proof, and we do not get told why you're chosen for your selected Purgatory.

Anything else? I have a lot to do as you can see,' Jonny said calmly, although he was beginning to get irritated.

She turned on her heel, saying nothing. She stormed out of the office, the door slamming behind her.

'Always a pleasure,' Jonny called after her.

Later on, Jonny had made some headway with the files in front of him, not to mention the archaic computer system. He had to admit, it may be ancient, but what it could actually do would astonish even Bill Gates. It truly was other-worldly. The amount of information it held, and what Jonny could find out about people, was truly epic. Big brother really is watching, he thought to himself with a smirk.

Whilst Jonny worked on the last but one file, there was a delicate knock on the door behind him. He turned, an eyebrow raised and said, 'Come on in.' His voice held a slight trepidation, as he never knew if it would be good or bad news coming.

Bob walked through the door, smiling.

His abnormally long body walked over to the desk, where he perched on the same seat that Amy had vacated earlier. The overhead lights reflection bounced off his large, bold head.

He was smiling confidently, which was rare, if nearly non-existent, Jonny thought.

'What's up, Bob?' Jonny asked nonchalantly.

Bob did not speak. His smile grew into a grin. He simply placed an item on the desk that he had been clutching, previously unnoticed by Jonny. He was clearly delighted with himself. 'You OK there, buddy?' Jonny asked with a small, hesitant laugh.

'A little gift for you, my friend.' Bob said at last, barely containing his glee.

It was a file, similar to all the others.

Bob tapped the file with his middle finger, several times, excitedly.

'Wow. Thanks Bob. Another file. My day couldn't get any better!' Jonny said sarcastically.

Bob looked confused momentarily, then laughed.

Jonny looked at him concerned. This was a Bob that Jonny had never met.

'Jonny... it's *the* file,' Bob said.

Jonny's breath caught in his throat. He nearly choked. 'It's ... *her* file?' he hissed, excitedly.

Bob nodded vigorously in response.

'Holy shit... this is... Autumn's papers? She really is leaving Purgatory?' Jonny stated, barely believing his own words.

'She is indeed, my friend. Also, just to help you out... I've ensured she will be in the same sector, and she will be working the same shifts as you. That way, when you're home,' he said, pointing upwards, 'you'll always be together.' He finished with a wide smile.

'Seriously, this is all definitely sorted?' Jonny asked, giddily.

'One hundred percent signed off, Jonny. Congratulations!' Bob replied, proudly.

A little later, after Bob had left, Jonny just sat for a long while relaxing in the chair.

He thought about everything that had been and everything that was to come. He had to admit, he was extremely excited. He was desperate to see Autumn again, even if it had only been a short while since they last saw each other.

He smiled to himself, leant over and picked up his cigarette pack. He removed one and lit it.

He inhaled deeply. It was his reward for a good day... a celebratory day.

Jonny frowned slightly then, realising he hadn't asked Bob an important question.

He got up, extinguished the smoke quickly, and walked purposefully towards the back door that Bob had exited earlier.

The corridor went on forever, or it felt like it did to Jonny.

He picked up his pace, knowing he was not far from the little alcove where Bob's desk was situated.

As he approached the area that Jonny knew Bob inhabited, he again eyed the subtle changes in décor, appreciatively. It seemed the roaring 1920's deeply influenced this area.

Bold coving on the ceilings and angled wall lights were commonplace.

Finally, he approached a big, grand set of double doors that had elaborate, brass handles.

Just to the right of them, was the alcove where Bob sat at his desk.

Bob was hunched over a computer keyboard, periodically looking up at the old screen. It was much like the one in Jonny's own office.

Jonny approached stealthily, then slapped his hand on top of the desk.

Bob literally jumped out of his chair with an overly high pitch yelp of surprise.

He swivelled his chair to face Jonny, his glasses slightly off kilter.

Jonny laughed and said, 'Sorry, buddy! Didn't mean to scare you!' A fake evil grin, adorning his lips.

'Prick,' Was all that Bob said. He grinned too then. 'Just as well I can't die!' he said, laughing.

'Too true!' Jonny exclaimed. 'Listen, Bob...' Jonny began, more seriously.

'I forgot to ask... I was so shocked when you came to see me, it never occurred to me to ask the obvious question. When will Autumn actually leave Purgatory?' Jonny asked, trepidation subtly echoing in his voice.

Bob grinned at Jonny. 'I'm all about efficiency, Jonny, you know that. I showed you the file just before I delivered it. She will be having her meeting with the manager, shortly. After that, you know the rest...' Bob said, smiling.

Jonny thought to himself and smiled widely at Bob. He knew what that meant, she would be ascending in no time at all.

Jonny frowned then, another question coming to the forefront of his mind.

'Hang on Bob... you said we would have the same schedules, right?' he queried.

'I did.' Bob replied, still smiling.

'Does that mean... my shift won't be lasting long?' Jonny asked, mentally crossing his fingers.

Bob grinned at Jonny in response. 'You got it in one, buddy! I've pulled some strings. This shift of yours is going to be very short indeed. By the time Autumn has settled in... up there... learnt the ropes and all that... you'll be off to meet her. You're welcome,' he said, a proud look on his features.

'We don't deserve you, Bob!' Jonny said, barely containing his excitement.

'No! You don't!' Bob replied with a laugh.

Suddenly a shrill, persistent ringing cut through the air, like a knife through butter.

Both Jonny and Bob looked down to the red phone, sitting on Bob's desk. A look of utter dread plastering both their faces, replacing the happy smiles of mere moments ago.

With a slight shake in his hand, Bob quickly picked up the phone's handset and listened.

Jonny held his breath; he knew the red phone ringing was never a good sign.

Shock followed by horror adorned Bob's features. After a moment of listening, he simply said, 'I understand. I'm on the way.'

He slammed the handset down, making the phone bells jingle.

He shot out of his chair, ready for action. Just as he was about to turn and head down the corridor, Jonny grabbed his arm. 'What is it, Bob?' Jonny asked in a scared voice.

'I gotta go, Jonny! It's your old diner!' he replied.

Jonny let go of his arm in shock. Bob patted Jonny on the shoulder, and then he was off, all but running down the corridor.

Over his shoulder, he shouted back to Jonny, 'Don't follow me, Jonny. You know you're not allowed!'

Jonny just stood there, dumfounded.

What the fuck was going on? He let out a yell of frustration.

He stormed back towards his own office. When he got there, he quickly walked over to the desk and sat heavily on the chair.

He grabbed his cigarettes and lit a smoke.

For what felt like an unimaginably long stretch of time, Jonny just sat, chain smoking.

His foot tapped subconsciously whilst he periodically looked over at the back door.

It could be anything, he thought to himself. 'So why are you so damn scared?' his inner voice asked him.

As a thousand-yard stare engrossed him, the door behind him suddenly swung open with no warning.

Bob walked in. He looked to be the ultimate example of desolate.

He all but fell into the chair opposite Jonny.

In growing dread, Jonny noticed that Bob had tears in his eyes.

'Bob... what the hell has happened?' Jonny asked, a quiver running through his voice.

He was sure he did not want to know the answer, yet he had to know.

Jonny's world fell apart then, as Bob replied in a whisper, 'Autumn... she's gone.'

He just stared at the man opposite him, who wouldn't

meet his gaze.

Jonny couldn't speak. He couldn't even breathe. Suddenly he took a gaping breath, tears began falling freely down his cheeks.

'What happened to her?' he croaked.

Bob took a while to answer. Finally, he spoke, hesitantly. 'You remember Hildegard, right?'

'The short, plump German woman,' Jonny replied quickly.

'Yes. Well... she left... ran out of the diner's exit...' Bob replied, trailing off at the end.

Jonny gestured with his hands, making a quick circling motion, meaning for Bob to hurry up.

Bob hesitated, looking increasingly nervous. He then blurted, 'She grabbed Autumn at an opportune moment, then pulled them both through the door! They're gone... I'm so sorry, buddy.'

Jonny felt like he'd been hit by a freight train. How could this have happened? The Devil was banished for Christ's sake!

Finally, Jonny spoke. 'This makes... no sense, Bob. Why would Hildegard do this?'

Bob looked utterly broken, he would not meet Jonny's hard gaze.

'There was a notebook... something that Hildegard always had with her. We reviewed it right away. She had kept a detailed diary in there for some time. It seems she had been groomed by Ray... the Gatekeeper... over some time. Hildegard... was his... plan B.' Bob finished, looking down at his hands.

Jonny just stared at the bowed head of Bob. The emotions of frustration and sympathy fighting each other in his mind.

'This still makes no sense at all.' Jonny said, controlling his voice.

'Her writings clearly show how she changed... how she began to believe that 'thing,' and it's manipulation to be gospel. Eventually it seems he told her his true identity... promised her everything she could want for... if she acted in a situation where he couldn't. The last notes were focused on you and Autumn, alone. It seemed the 'thing' took a particular dislike to you... the writings stated you must be destroyed... by destroying what is most important to you.' Bob finished, his words quickly spilling out as if to rid him of these terrible thoughts.

Jonny tried to focus. He would not let his mind stray at such a pivotal point.

'The Devil must have been concerned that things could go array. It clearly thought that I would have something to do with it. Regardless, it wanted me to suffer whether it was my fault or not that it's plans went south.' Jonny said to himself as much as Bob.

Bob simply nodded in agreement. Bob stood slowly then; he rustled in his trouser pocket for a moment. Delicately, he placed something on the desk in front of Jonny.

He recognised it instantly by the flowers and unicorns that adorned the edges. It was *their* note.

Jonny held back a sob as Bob slowly walked round the desk. He placed a hand on Jonny's shoulder.

'I'm so sorry, Jonny. None of us thought this was possible. Wendy... or should I say the Gatekeeper of Paradise... met me there... she can't believe it either.' he said, apologetically.

In a voice that was softer still, Bob gingerly spoke, 'There's... nothing any of us can do, Jonny. I'm truly sorry. She's gone... forever.'

With that, the sobs erupted from Jonny, spilling out like a dam finally breaking.

He placed his head on the desk and covered his ears, not wanting to hear anymore.

The noises coming from Jonny resembled a wounded animal. Bob quietly left the office, leaving Jonny to his misery.

In his tight-fisted hand, Jonny held on to the note. He read the text he had scrawled with one bleary eye, now knowing it would never come to fruition.

'I couldn't say goodbye as I'll never say it again. That I pledge to you. I love you. I cannot wait to be beside you once again.'